BOOK 8 OF THE
ADULT LEARNER SERIES

Peril on the Road

JUDITH ANDREWS GREEN
DIRECTOR,
OXFORD HILLS ADULT AND
COMMUNITY EDUCATION
SCHOOL ADMINISTRATIVE DISTRICT #17
SOUTH PARIS, MAINE

JAMESTOWN PUBLISHERS
PROVIDENCE, RHODE ISLAND

Catalog No. 207

Peril on the Road

Cover and Story Illustrations by
Bob Giuliani

Printed in the United States AL

88 89 90 9 8 7 6 5 4 3 2

ISBN 0-89061-427-X

Titles in the Series

No. 200, Murder by Radio
No. 201, The Man Who Stopped Time
No. 202, The Man with the Scar
No. 203, Dr. Valdez
No. 204, The Secret of Room 401
No. 205, A City for Ransom
No. 206, Nightmare Snow
No. 207, Peril on the Road
No. 208, Killer in a Trance?

To my best beloved
Roger

To the Reader

Jeff and Rita were going across the country on a motorcycle for their honeymoon. That was all. Just the two of them and their little dog, Mop.

Then they found themselves following two men in a van. Or were the men following them? You will find out as you read the chapters of *Peril on the Road.*

Before each chapter of the story, there are words for you to read and learn. The words are given in sentences, so that you can see how they will be used in the story. After each chapter, there are questions for you to answer. The questions will give you an idea of how well you are reading.

Also following each chapter is a section called Language Skills. It has lessons that will help you to read, write and spell better.

The last two parts of each unit deal with Life Skills. Life Skills are things you need to know about and know how to do to get along in life.

The answers to all the questions and exercises are in the back of the book. You can check your answers to see if they are right.

We hope you will like reading *Peril on the Road* and learning all the things this book teaches.

Contents

How to Use This Book

Preview Words/*Chapter 1*

Study the words in the box. Then read the sentences below with your teacher. Look carefully at the words in boldface type.

area	crawled	married	saddlebags
apartment	followed	motorcycle	signal
breakfast	gleaming	packages	touring
clothes	heavy	presents	traffic
country	honeymoon	relax	wondered

1. It was the biggest day of their lives—the day they were getting **married**.
2. You can't go all that way on a **motorcycle**!
3. He has a nice **apartment** in San Francisco.
4. They cut the wedding cake and opened their wedding **presents**.
5. Jeff and Rita changed their **clothes**.
6. Their gear was packed in the bike's **saddlebags**.
7. Jeff flashed the turn **signal**.
8. He turned the motorcycle into a highway rest **area**.
9. The motorcycle stood **gleaming** in the light from the fire.
10. They **followed** the signs to the campground.
11. This is a **touring** bike, a Yamaha XL 750.
12. Oh **relax**, Ken, I didn't tell them anything.
13. They just got married and they're on their **honeymoon**.
14. They're going across the **country** on that bike.
15. The two men sat down to eat their **breakfast**.
16. Jeff **crawled** out of the tent.
17. There wasn't much **traffic** on the highway.
18. The van must have a **heavy** load.
19. Jeff **wondered** why they were going so fast.
20. All he could see was a lot of big, flat **packages**.

00 PERIL ON THE ROAD

1. Learn the Preview Words

Say the words in the box. Then read the sentences. Try to learn the words. See if you know what each sentence means.

On the Road/*Chapter 1*

The big day had come at last. It was the biggest day of their lives—the day they were getting married and the day they were setting out on their big trip. Today they would leave New York City, and in two weeks they would be in California.

Jeff and Rita had been planning for this day for a long time. Well, Rita's mother had been planning for it, too. She had made all the plans for the wedding. Jeff and Rita had spent all their time thinking about the trip to California.

"You're crazy!" Rita's mother kept telling them. "You can't do it! You can't go all the way across the United States—not on a motorcycle! You'll never make it! You'll never even get out of New York City!"

"Sure we will, Mom," Rita kept telling her. "We've got it all planned, and we have two weeks to do it in. Don't worry about us."

"Don't worry? That's easy for you to say! Two crazy kids on a motorcycle. And a dog!"

"Mom," Rita would say in a tired voice, "we're not kids. We know what we're doing. Jeff has two weeks off before he has to get back to his job. He has a nice apartment waiting for us, so when we get to San Francisco we'll be all set. I'm sure I'll find a job right away, too. We've taken lots of short trips on the bike. We've taken Mop on some short trips too. She loves it. So we know what we're doing. Now come on, Mom, we've been through this over and over. There's nothing to worry about."

But Rita's mother would start right in again. "All the

ON THE ROAD 00

2. Read the Chapter

As you read, try to follow the events of the story. See if you can figure out what the "peril," or danger is.

Comprehension Questions/*Chapter 1*

Directions. Answer these questions about the chapter you have just read. Put an x in the box beside the best answer to each question.

1. (B) Where were Jeff and Rita going on their trip?
   - ☐ a. New York City
   - ☐ b. San Francisco
   - ☐ c. New Jersey
   - ☐ d. Utah

2. (B) How did Jeff and Rita carry Mop on the motorcycle?
   - ☐ a. In the saddlebag
   - ☐ b. In Jeff's jacket
   - ☐ c. In Rita's jacket
   - ☐ d. On the seat

3. (E) What was the main reason Jeff and Rita were taking the trip?
   - ☐ a. It was the only way they could get to California.
   - ☐ b. Jeff wanted to show Rita how to ride a motorcycle.
   - ☐ c. They just wanted to take Mop for a ride.
   - ☐ d. They wanted to have a nice honeymoon trip.

COMPREHENSION QUESTIONS

3. Answer: Comprehension Questions

Put an x in the box next to the best answer to each question. Read all ten questions first and answer the easy ones. Then go back and answer the hard ones.

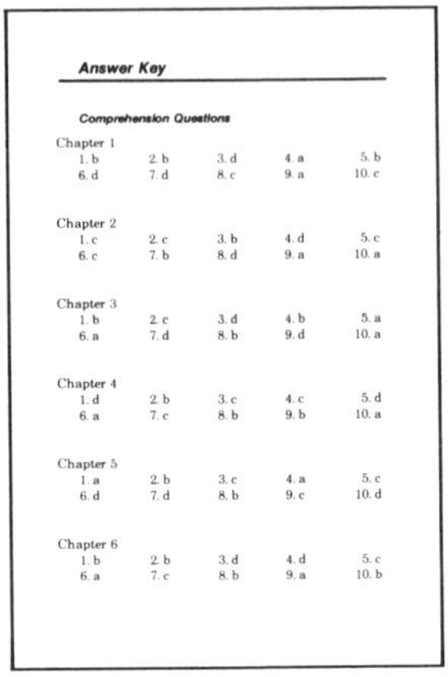

Answer Key

Comprehension Questions

Chapter					
Chapter 1	1. b	2. b	3. d	4. a	5. b
	6. d	7. d	8. c	9. a	10. c
Chapter 2	1. c	2. c	3. b	4. d	5. c
	6. c	7. b	8. d	9. a	10. a
Chapter 3	1. b	2. c	3. d	4. b	5. a
	6. a	7. d	8. b	9. d	10. a
Chapter 4	1. d	2. b	3. c	4. c	5. d
	6. a	7. c	8. b	9. b	10. a
Chapter 5	1. a	2. b	3. c	4. a	5. c
	6. d	7. d	8. b	9. c	10. d
Chapter 6	1. b	2. b	3. d	4. d	5. c
	6. a	7. c	8. b	9. a	10. b

4. *Correct Your Answers*

Use the Answer Key on page 240. Circle any answers you got wrong, and mark the right answers with an *x*.

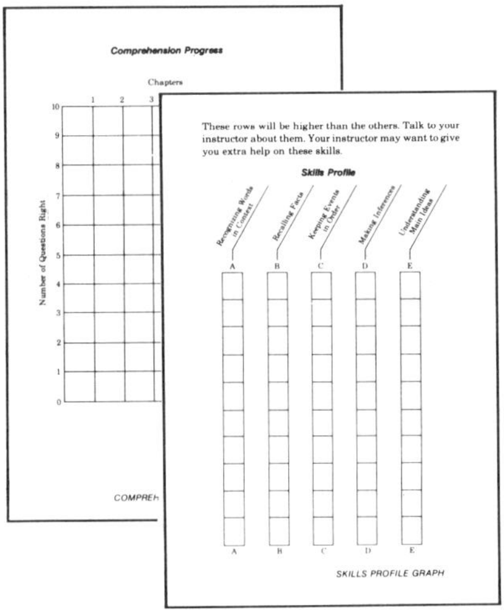

5. *Fill in the Graphs*

Fill in the graph on page 251 to show your comprehension score. Use the graph on page 253 to chart your skills.

6. *Read: Language Skills*

This comes after the questions. Read the pages and do the exercises. Use the Answer Key that begins on page 241 to correct the exercises.

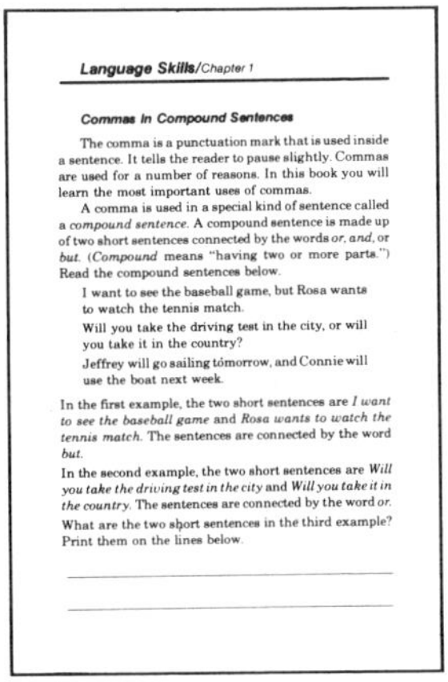

Language Skills/*Chapter 1*

Commas in Compound Sentences

The comma is a punctuation mark that is used inside a sentence. It tells the reader to pause slightly. Commas are used for a number of reasons. In this book you will learn the most important uses of commas.

A comma is used in a special kind of sentence called a *compound sentence*. A compound sentence is made up of two short sentences connected by the words *or*, *and*, or *but*. (*Compound* means "having two or more parts.") Read the compound sentences below.

I want to see the baseball game, but Rosa wants to watch the tennis match.

Will you take the driving test in the city, or will you take it in the country?

Jeffrey will go sailing tomorrow, and Connie will use the boat next week.

In the first example, the two short sentences are *I want to see the baseball game* and *Rosa wants to watch the tennis match*. The sentences are connected by the word *but*.

In the second example, the two short sentences are *Will you take the driving test in the city* and *Will you take it in the country*. The sentences are connected by the word *or*.

What are the two short sentences in the third example? Print them on the lines below.

7. *Read: Understanding Life Skills*

Read these pages and follow the step-by-step lessons. Use the Answer Key that begins on page 246 to check your answers.

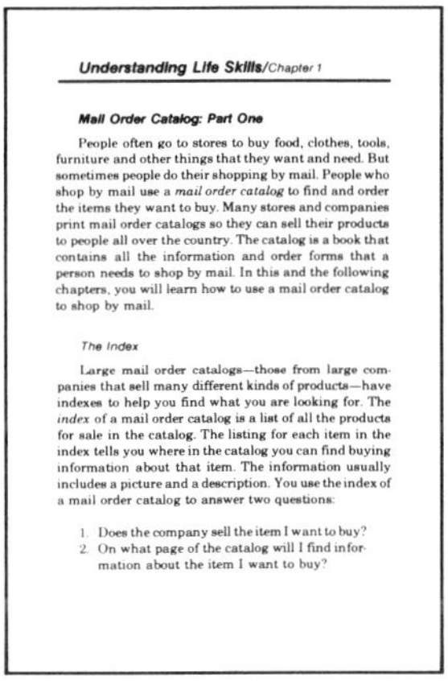

Understanding Life Skills/*Chapter 1*

Mail Order Catalog: Part One

People often go to stores to buy food, clothes, tools, furniture and other things that they want and need. But sometimes people do their shopping by mail. People who shop by mail use a *mail order catalog* to find and order the items they want to buy. Many stores and companies print mail order catalogs so they can sell their products to people all over the country. The catalog is a book that contains all the information and order forms that a person needs to shop by mail. In this and the following chapters, you will learn how to use a mail order catalog to shop by mail.

The Index

Large mail order catalogs—those from large companies that sell many different kinds of products—have indexes to help you find what you are looking for. The *index* of a mail order catalog is a list of all the products for sale in the catalog. The listing for each item in the index tells you where in the catalog you can find buying information about that item. The information usually includes a picture and a description. You use the index of a mail order catalog to answer two questions:

1. Does the company sell the item I want to buy?
2. On what page of the catalog will I find information about the item I want to buy?

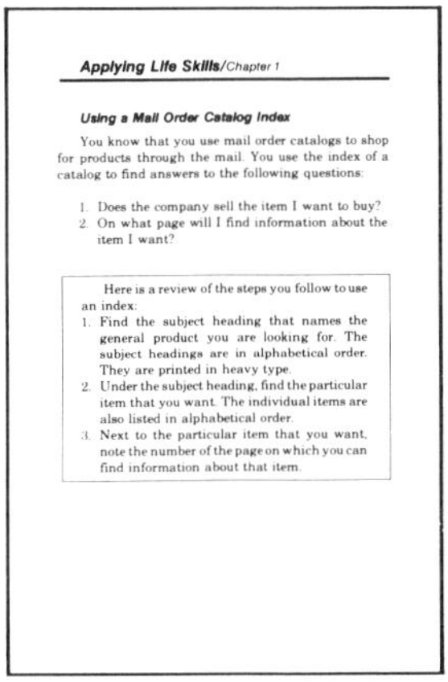

Applying Life Skills/*Chapter 1*

Using a Mail Order Catalog Index

You know that you use mail order catalogs to shop for products through the mail. You use the index of a catalog to find answers to the following questions:

1. Does the company sell the item I want to buy?
2. On what page will I find information about the item I want?

Here is a review of the steps you follow to use an index:
1. Find the subject heading that names the general product you are looking for. The subject headings are in alphabetical order. They are printed in heavy type.
2. Under the subject heading, find the particular item that you want. The individual items are also listed in alphabetical order.
3. Next to the particular item that you want, note the number of the page on which you can find information about that item.

8. *Practice: Applying Life Skills*

Read the instructions and do the Life Skills exercise. Take your time. Do the work carefully. Try to remember what you just read about understanding life skills. Use the Answer Key that begins on page 247 to correct the exercise.

9. *Read the Chapter Again*

Go back to the story and read it once more. This time as you read, try to feel all the interest and excitement the writer has built in.

Then go to the Preview Words for the next chapter.

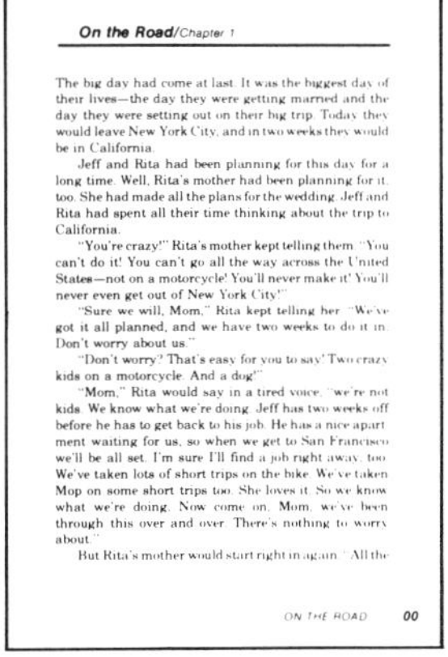

On the Road/*Chapter 1*

The big day had come at last. It was the biggest day of their lives—the day they were getting married and the day they were setting out on their big trip. Today they would leave New York City, and in two weeks they would be in California.

Jeff and Rita had been planning for this day for a long time. Well, Rita's mother had been planning for it, too. She had made all the plans for the wedding. Jeff and Rita had spent all their time thinking about the trip to California.

"You're crazy!" Rita's mother kept telling them. "You can't do it! You can't go all the way across the United States—not on a motorcycle! You'll never make it! You'll never even get out of New York City!"

"Sure we will, Mom," Rita kept telling her. "We've got it all planned, and we have two weeks to do it in. Don't worry about us."

"Don't worry? That's easy for you to say! Two crazy kids on a motorcycle. And a dog!"

"Mom," Rita would say in a tired voice, "we're not kids. We know what we're doing. Jeff has two weeks off before he has to get back to his job. He has a nice apartment waiting for us, so when we get to San Francisco we'll be all set. I'm sure I'll find a job right away, too. We've taken lots of short trips on the bike. We've taken Mop on some short trips too. She loves it. So we know what we're doing. Now come on, Mom, we've been through this over and over. There's nothing to worry about."

But Rita's mother would start right in again. "All the

ON THE ROAD 00

1

On the Road

Preview Words/*Chapter 1*

Study the words in the box. Then read the sentences below with your teacher. Look carefully at the words in boldface type.

area	crawled	married	saddlebags
apartment	followed	motorcycle	signal
breakfast	gleaming	packages	touring
clothes	heavy	presents	traffic
country	honeymoon	relax	wondered

1. It was the biggest day of their lives—the day they were getting **married**.
2. You can't go all that way on a **motorcycle**!
3. He has a nice **apartment** in San Francisco.
4. They cut the wedding cake and opened their wedding **presents**.
5. Jeff and Rita changed their **clothes**.
6. Their gear was packed in the bike's **saddlebags**.
7. Jeff flashed the turn **signal**.
8. He turned the motorcycle into a highway rest **area**.
9. The motorcycle stood **gleaming** in the light from the fire.
10. They **followed** the signs to the campground.
11. This is a **touring** bike, a Yamaha XL 750.
12. Oh **relax**, Ken, I didn't tell them anything.
13. They just got married and they're on their **honeymoon**.
14. They're going across the **country** on that bike.
15. The two men sat down to eat their **breakfast**.
16. Jeff **crawled** out of the tent.
17. There wasn't much **traffic** on the highway.
18. The van must have a **heavy** load.
19. Jeff **wondered** why they were going so fast.
20. All he could see was a lot of big, flat **packages**.

The big day had come at last. It was the biggest day of their lives—the day they were getting married and the day they were setting out on their big trip. Today they would leave New York City, and in two weeks they would be in California.

Jeff and Rita had been planning for this day for a long time. Well, Rita's mother had been planning for it, too. She had made all the plans for the wedding. Jeff and Rita had spent all their time thinking about the trip to California.

"You're crazy!" Rita's mother kept telling them. "You can't do it! You can't go all the way across the United States—not on a motorcycle! You'll never make it! You'll never even get out of New York City!"

"Sure we will, Mom," Rita kept telling her. "We've got it all planned, and we have two weeks to do it in. Don't worry about us."

"Don't worry? That's easy for you to say! Two crazy kids on a motorcycle. And a dog!"

"Mom," Rita would say in a tired voice, "we're not kids. We know what we're doing. Jeff has two weeks off before he has to get back to his job. He has a nice apartment waiting for us, so when we get to San Francisco we'll be all set. I'm sure I'll find a job right away, too. We've taken lots of short trips on the bike. We've taken Mop on some short trips too. She loves it. So we know what we're doing. Now come on, Mom, we've been through this over and over. There's nothing to worry about."

But Rita's mother would start right in again. "All the

way across the United States, on a motorcycle, with a dog!"

"Now, Mom, you know that Mop isn't just a dog. Mop is more like a person."

Mop would pick up her ears when she heard her name. She would run over and stand by Rita's feet, barking. The little dog had such long hair that no one could tell which end was her head and which end was her tail. She looked just like a little dust mop.

Rita would pick her up and pat her, saying, "Don't worry, Mop, you're coming with us on the big trip."

And Rita's mother would walk away, shaking her head.

Now it was Saturday afternoon—the big day had come. The wedding went well. All their friends and family were at the church. Jeff was grinning from ear to ear, and Rita felt so happy that she wanted to cry. Mop just ran around in a big pink ribbon, getting in the way. After the wedding, everyone stayed to eat and drink. Rita and Jeff cut the wedding cake and opened their wedding presents.

At last it was time to go.

Jeff and Rita changed their clothes. They looked funny in their blue jeans and boots and black leather jackets, standing there with people who were all dressed up for the wedding. "We look as if we don't belong here," Jeff laughed.

"So, let's go!" Rita said.

They walked out the back door of the church. There, in the middle of the parking lot, stood Jeff's motorcycle, with all their gear packed into its saddlebags. They were ready to go.

"Crazy! Crazy!" Rita's mother said.

"Don't worry, Mom," Rita said, "we'll send you a

postcard from every place we stop." She gave her mother a hug, then looked around and called, "Come on, Mop!"

Mop came running. She still had the big ribbon she had worn for the wedding. Now she stopped and pulled it off. Then she jumped up onto the seat of the motorcycle. "Good girl," Jeff said. He unzipped his jacket part of the way and popped Mop into it. Mop curled up in the jacket with her head sticking out under Jeff's chin.

Jeff and Rita put their helmets on their heads. Jeff got onto the motorcycle, and Rita climbed up behind him, leaning back against the sissy bar. Jeff started the motor.

"Good-bye!"

"Have a good trip!"

"Drive carefully!"

"Good-bye!"

Everyone was shouting as Jeff and Rita drove out of

the parking lot. Over all the rest, Rita's mother could be heard shouting, "Crazy! You're both crazy! *All three of you* are crazy!"

They drove through the streets of New York City. Rita had lived there all her life, but now everything looked strange. She was leaving—leaving her home and going to a strange city three thousand miles away.

She wished that she could talk to Jeff about it. But he couldn't really hear her over the sound of the motor and the wind rushing by, and she wouldn't get him to pull over for something like that. She wished that she had Mop in her jacket. Mop always knew how she felt. Mop could always cheer her up.

Soon they were out of New York City. Now that they were on the open highway, Rita forgot to feel sad. They were on their way!

The miles went by quickly. Suddenly Jeff waved his arm, and Rita looked to see what he was pointing at. It was a big sign that said

WELCOME TO NEW JERSEY

Rita hugged Jeff around the waist. It was a big moment. They weren't in New York anymore. They were in a new state. They had crossed their first state line!

How many state lines would they have to cross? How many states before they got to California? Rita tried to count them in her head, but she gave up after a while. She was happy just to ride along and watch New Jersey go by.

Jeff flashed his turn signal and turned into a highway rest area. They rode across the parking lot, slowing to a stop. As the bike stopped, they swung their left legs out at the same moment. "It feels as if we've been doing this for years," Rita thought proudly.

Jeff put down the kickstand. It felt so good to stand

up and take off their helmets. Jeff gave Rita a hug, but Mop popped her head up between them and barked, making them both laugh.

Jeff put Mop down on the ground, and she ran off to look around. Jeff and Rita walked slowly around the rest area with their arms around each other. "How are you holding up?" Jeff asked.

"Oh I'm fine," Rita said. "Just a little tired. It's been a big day."

"It sure has!" Jeff gave Rita another hug. "The best day of my life. But we'll stop for the night soon. We'll stop at the first campground we see, OK?"

"It sounds good to me!" Rita said.

When Rita called to Mop, the little dog came running back and hopped around Jeff's feet. "Look at her!" Jeff said. "She's always ready to go." He picked her up and put her back in his jacket.

They got back on the bike and pulled out of the parking lot. As they got back on the highway, Rita leaned back against the sissy bar. She felt so tired. What a day!

Before long they passed a sign that read

FOOD GAS

CAMPING

NEXT EXIT

Jeff pointed to the sign, and Rita saw the turn signal come on. A campground at last!

They took the exit off the highway and followed the signs to the campground. They checked in at the campground office, then rode slowly around the campground, looking for a good campsite.

They found a campsite that looked out over a river. They parked the bike and walked over to the river. They stood there for a moment, holding hands, not talking.

Then Jeff said, "Let's set up camp."

First they set up their little tent. Jeff got a fire going while Rita got out the food, and soon their supper was cooking over the fire.

They ate their supper, then sat by the fire as it got dark. Mop ran about here and there, checking out all the strange new smells. The only sounds were the crackling fire and the river running by. "Happy?" Jeff asked.

"I've never been so happy," Rita said. "It's so peaceful here."

Just then a van came down the road. "I hope they don't stop near us," Jeff said. But the van pulled into the campsite next to them, and two men got out. While one of the men opened the back of the van and pulled out sleeping bags and boxes of food, the other man started a fire.

Rita and Jeff tried to get back the feeling of peace that they had had before the van came. They looked into their campfire and talked quietly. But Mop ran over to check out the new people.

Soon one of the men walked over to Jeff and Rita and asked, "Is that your dog? It sure is a cute little thing. I don't know if I've ever seen such a little dog. It's friendly, too."

"Yes, she likes everyone," Rita said. "Her name is Mop."

The man laughed. "She does look like a mop, doesn't she! Does she ride on the bike with you?"

"Yes, she rides in Jeff's jacket."

The man walked over to the motorcycle, which stood gleaming in the light from the fire. He walked all the way around the bike, looking at it carefully, with his hands stuck into his back pockets. "This is quite a bike!" he said.

Jeff got up and walked over to him. "I like it," he said.

"It's a touring bike, a Yamaha XL 750. We're going across the United States on it, all the way to San Francisco." Rita came over and stood beside him, and he put his arm around her. "This is my wife, Rita—we just got married today. My name is Jeff."

"Well, well, glad to meet you. My name is Steve," the man said, shaking Jeff's hand, then Rita's. "I hope to get a bike like this someday. I hope someone like you comes with it," he added, winking at Rita. Rita turned away and went to find Mop.

"How long are you going to be on the road?" Steve asked Jeff.

"Two weeks," Jeff told him. "Right now we're on our way to Chicago. We'll stop there for a few days so Rita can see her aunt and uncle. Then we'll head out through Iowa and Nebraska, then Wyoming—I want to do some camping there. Then we'll ride right through Utah and Nevada and on into California."

"Right across the United States!" Steve said. "Too bad you can't take some side trips and really see things."

"Well, I have to get back to work," Jeff said. "I have only two weeks off."

Steve was walking around the motorcycle again. "I've never really looked at a touring bike before," he told Jeff. "How does it ride?"

"Really great, even with two people and all our stuff on it. It has a lot of power, even going up hills. It—"

"Hey, Steve," the other man yelled from the van, "are you going to talk all night? Let's eat!"

"I've got to go," Steve told Jeff. "Have a good trip."

"Thanks. See you later."

Jeff walked back to the campfire, where Rita was sitting with Mop in her lap. "That Steve seemed like a really nice guy," Jeff said.

"I didn't think so," Rita said.

"Oh come on," Jeff said, sitting down next to Rita and putting his arm around her. "You always let people get to you." Rita didn't say anything, but she curled up against Jeff and leaned her head on him. The fire glowed on their faces and on Mop's fur.

In the next camp, the two men sat by their campfire eating. Steve kept looking over at the motorcycle. "That's some bike," he said at last.

"So what?" the other man asked sharply. "What was the big idea of going over there and getting so friendly with them? What did you tell them? What if they come over here and start looking around? What will happen then? Did you think of that?"

"Oh relax, Ken, I didn't tell them anything, and they won't be coming over here. They want to be alone—they just got married today. They're on their honeymoon. The guy told me all about their trip. They're going right across the country on that bike, all the way to San Francisco."

"San Francisco? Did you tell them that we're going to San Francisco too?"

"No, of course not. I told you I didn't tell them a thing."

"All right," Ken growled, "but just keep away from people, will you? We've got a long way to go, and we don't want anyone looking at us too closely."

"Yes, OK. Just relax," Steve said as he set down his plate and stretched his arms. "But you know what I'm going to do with part of my share of the money? I'm going to buy one of those touring bikes."

"Well we've got to get to San Francisco first. Now let's get some sleep. I want to be a long way from New York City when that place opens up on Monday."

They rolled their sleeping bags out on the ground

and got into them. Soon they were asleep. In the next campsite, Jeff and Rita still sat looking into the fire.

* * * * *

The next morning, as soon as it got light, the two men from the van got up and rolled up their sleeping bags. Ken opened the back of the van and got out one of the food boxes. The two men sat down by the coals of their fire to eat their breakfast.

In the next campsite, Mop woke up. She heard people moving around. They were eating! Food!

Mop barked to be let out of the tent. Sleepily, Jeff reached over and unzipped the tent. "Be a good girl, Mop," he said, "and don't get lost."

Mop hopped over him and ran out of the tent. She ran right over to the other campsite and sniffed around the two men. "Hello, Mop," Steve said. "Did you come to share our breakfast? Here, you can have a little of mine."

Get that mutt out of here!" Ken said. "I don't like to have dogs around while I'm eating." He kicked at Mop, and she ran around to the other side of the van. The two men went on eating.

Mop sniffed around the van. Food . . . There was a box on the ground next to the van. She stuck her head into it, but everything in the box was closed tightly. She climbed up on the box, then up onto the back bumper, so that she could stick her head into the van. Food . . . She climbed into the van and sniffed around some boxes and some big flat packages.

"Are you finished eating?" Ken asked Steve. "Then let's go!" He grabbed the box that was on the ground and threw it into the van. Steve threw the sleeping bags in on top and slammed the doors shut, then ran to get in the front of the van. Ken had already started the motor.

Just as the van pulled out of the campsite, Jeff crawled out of his tent. He waved good-bye to Steve, then walked down to look at the river. Rita crawled out of the tent, stretching her arms and yawning. She looked around for Mop, calling, "Mop, come here, girl! Time for breakfast!"

Mop did not come.

Rita looked around the campsite. She bent down and looked in the tent again, then looked down the road. "Jeff," she called, "is Mop down there by the river with you?"

"No, she isn't." Jeff walked back up to the campsite, saying, "She was here just a minute ago. Let's see . . . I let her out of the tent, and I could hear her sniffing around. Then I heard Steve and his friend packing up the van . . ."

"The van!" Rita ran over to the campsite where the van had been. "Look, Mop was over here!" she called to Jeff. "I can see her footprints. They go right up to where the van was parked, and then they stop! Oh, Jeff, she must be in the van!"

"Now, Rita," Jeff said, walking over to her, "why would those men want to steal Mop?"

"I don't mean that! You know how Mop likes to get into things! She must have got into the van, and then they drove away. "They never even saw her! Oh, Jeff, we've got to go after them! We've got to get her back!"

"But they've been gone for a while, and we don't even know which way they went! And—Where are you going?" Jeff called.

Rita was running toward the motorcycle. "I'm going after them!"

"No, wait!" Jeff ran after Rita. "Let me go! I know the bike a lot better than you do! Get off! It will go a lot faster with just one of us on it. And Mop may still be around here somewhere. You stay and look for her. Look down by the river." Jeff put on his helmet and jumped onto the motorcycle. He started it quickly and roared out onto the campground road, headed for the highway.

If only he knew which way they had gone! Well, he would just have to get on the highway and hope for the best. He had to try. The way Rita cared about that dog . . . Sometimes he felt as if she loved the dog more than she loved him!

Which way should he go? Without really thinking about it, he took the way that he and Rita would be going. He roared onto the highway, going west.

That early in the morning, there wasn't much traffic. Jeff hoped that there wouldn't be any cops. 65 . . . 70 . . . 75 . . . He opened up the bike and let it roar down the road. It was a great ride. It felt so good to open the bike up and see what it would do that he almost forgot about watching for the van.

Suddenly he saw it, way up ahead. He roared down the road after it. The van wasn't going very fast. They must have a heavy load, Jeff thought. He was closing in quickly. But suddenly the van was going faster. Why did they speed up? Jeff wondered. It didn't matter—the van was no match for his bike.

He rode up next to the van and waved for the driver to pull over. At first the driver wouldn't do it. Jeff could see him talking to Steve. Then, at last, he pulled over.

Jeff parked his bike in front of the van. As he walked toward the van, Steve rolled down his window and asked, "What's up?"

"My wife's dog," Jeff said. "We think she's in the back of your van. She's always getting into things like that. I just want to take a look."

"No, wait!" Steve shouted, but Jeff was already walking around to the back of the van. He opened the door and looked inside.

All he could see was a lot of big, flat packages, all done up in brown paper, with rope around them. They were standing up, leaning against the sides of the van. There were the sleeping bags, too, and some clothes. But no Mop.

"Steve and Ken came running around the side of the van. "What do you think you're doing?" Ken shouted.

"I'm just looking for our dog," Jeff said, sticking his head into the van again and looking into a corner. There was a box of food he hadn't seen before. And there was Mop, fast asleep.

"There you are!" Jeff said, grabbing her and pulling her out of the van. He held her up to show the two men, saying, "My wife was right. She was after your food. Sorry about that." He put Mop into the front of his jacket and got back on his bike. "I'm sorry I had to stop you like that. Have a good trip. See you later," he called to the two men. Then he carefully rode across the grass in the middle of the highway and roared back toward the campground.

Steve and Ken watched him go. Then Ken closed the back of the van. "What do you think?" he asked Steve. "Was he really just looking for the dog, or was he looking for something else?"

"Relax," Steve said. "He was just getting his dog. They weren't even up yet when we left, so he couldn't have *put* the dog in there."

"Well, what was the idea of leaving these doors unlocked? He just walked back here and opened them up!"

"You didn't give me time to lock them! You were in such a hurry to go!" Steve said.

"But he saw *everything!*" Ken shouted.

"Relax, just relax. You'll never make it to California if you worry about every guy in every campground," Steve said as he got back into the van.

Ken checked the doors again, then got into the van too. "All right," he told Steve, "but I'm going to be watching for that guy. And if I see him again—"

By that time, Jeff was pulling into the campground. Rita ran up to him as he pulled into the campsite, calling, "Did you find the van? Did you find Mop?" Jeff unzipped his jacket, and Mop jumped out. "Oh, Mop," Rita said, "you bad dog, getting into that van and making poor Jeff go look for those men."

"They were really nice about it," Jeff said. "They didn't mind at all, so don't worry about a thing. I had a really good ride, too," he added, giving Rita a hug.

As they sat down to eat their breakfast, Jeff said, "You know, those men are headed the same way we are. I wonder if we'll see them again?"

Comprehension Questions*/Chapter 1*

Directions. Answer these questions about the chapter you have just read. Put an *x* in the box beside the best answer to each question.

1. (B) Where were Jeff and Rita going on their trip?

- ☐ a. New York City
- ☐ b. San Francisco
- ☐ c. New Jersey
- ☐ d. Utah

2. (B) How did Jeff and Rita carry Mop on the motorcycle?

- ☐ a. In the saddlebag
- ☐ b. In Jeff's jacket
- ☐ c. In Rita's jacket
- ☐ d. On the seat

3. (E) What was the main reason Jeff and Rita were taking the trip?

- ☐ a. It was the only way they could get to California.
- ☐ b. Jeff wanted to show Rita how to ride a motorcycle.
- ☐ c. They just wanted to take Mop for a ride.
- ☐ d. They wanted to have a nice honeymoon trip.

4. (D) Why was Rita's mother so worried?

- ☐ a. She felt that Jeff and Rita were too young and motorcycles too dangerous for such a trip.
- ☐ b. She didn't want Rita to marry Jeff.
- ☐ c. She knew that Jeff didn't know how to drive.
- ☐ d. She didn't want to lose Mop.

5. (C) What did Rita and Jeff do first?

- ☐ a. They changed their clothes.
- ☐ b. They cut the wedding cake.
- ☐ c. They left New York City.
- ☐ d. They rode out of the parking lot.

6. (A) When they stopped, Jeff asked Rita, *"How are you holding up?"* What did he mean?

- ☐ a. Can you sit all right?
- ☐ b. Can you hold Mop?
- ☐ c. Can you carry the saddlebag?
- ☐ d. Are you getting tired?

7. (E) What is the most important thing that happened to Rita and Jeff on the first part of their trip?

- ☐ a. They stopped at a campground.
- ☐ b. They crossed a state line.
- ☐ c. They packed up the motorcycle.
- ☐ d. They met the men in the van.

8. (A) Jeff knew that *the van was no match for his bike.* What does this mean?

- ☐ a. The van was not on fire.
- ☐ b. The van didn't look like the motorcycle.
- ☐ c. The van couldn't go as fast as the motorcycle.
- ☐ d. The van was faster than the motorcycle.

9. (C) Which of the following happened last?

- ☐ a. Jeff found Mop in the back of the van.
- ☐ b. The van pulled out of the campground.
- ☐ c. Jeff saw the van ahead of him on the highway.
- ☐ d. Jeff let Mop out of the tent.

10. (D) Why didn't the two men want Jeff to open the back of the van?

- ☐ a. They didn't want him to find Mop.
- ☐ b. They were afraid he would break the doors.
- ☐ c. They didn't want him to see what they had in the van.
- ☐ d. They knew that the doors were locked.

Skills Used to Answer Questions

A. Recognizing Words in Context B. Recalling Facts
C. Keeping Events in Order D. Making Inferences
E. Understanding Main Ideas

Commas in Compound Sentences

The comma is a punctuation mark that is used inside a sentence. It tells the reader to pause slightly. Commas are used for a number of reasons. In this book you will learn the most important uses of commas.

A comma is used in a special kind of sentence called a *compound sentence.* A compound sentence is made up of two short sentences connected by the words *or, and,* or *but.* (*Compound* means "having two or more parts.") Read the compound sentences below.

> I want to see the baseball game, but Rosa wants to watch the tennis match.
>
> Will you take the driving test in the city, or will you take it in the country?
>
> Jeffrey will go sailing tomorrow, and Connie will use the boat next week.

In the first example, the two short sentences are *I want to see the baseball game* and *Rosa wants to watch the tennis match.* The sentences are connected by the word *but.*

In the second example, the two short sentences are *Will you take the driving test in the city* and *Will you take it in the country.* The sentences are connected by the word *or.*

What are the two short sentences in the third example? Print them on the lines below.

____

____

What word connects those two sentences? ____________

Now look back at the three examples to see where the comma belongs in a compound sentence. You can see that it is placed just before the connecting word *or, and,* or *but.* The comma tells you to pause slightly between the two parts of the compound sentence.

Exercise 1

The compound sentences below have no commas. Print each sentence on the lines provided, putting the comma where it belongs. Remember that the comma in a compound sentence goes just before the connecting word. The first sentence has been done for you as an example.

1. The Smiths have a new baby girl and the Greenbergs have a baby boy.

   The Smiths have a new baby girl, and the Greenbergs have a baby boy.

2. We are eating chicken at the picnic and they are eating hamburgers.

   ____

   ____

   ____

3. Are you moving into your new house on Saturday or will you wait until Monday?

4. Cara wanted to take a trip to Florida but she did not have enough money.

5. I will get the tools and Janice will change the oil in my car.

6. Beverly waited a few more minutes and then she decided to go on by herself.

7. I would like to take the children to the zoo but I have to work this weekend.

____

____

____

8. Andy will visit you on Sunday and Sam will drop by on Monday.

____

____

____

Making Your Own Compound Sentences

The two parts of a compound sentence are closely related. In other words, their ideas go together. You can make compound sentences by connecting two short sentences with the joining words *or, and,* or *but*. Look at the examples below.

I have only one dog. ↓ I have three cats.

I have only one dog, <u>but</u> I have three cats.

Will Peter go in his own car? ↓ Will he ride with us?

Will Peter go in his own car, <u>or</u> will he ride with us?

You can see that each compound sentence has a comma. Where is the comma placed in each sentence? What does the comma tell you to do?

Exercise 2

Below are nine pairs of short sentences. Make each pair into a compound sentence by connecting the two short sentences. Connect the sentences with the word that is given next to them. Be sure to put a comma where it belongs in each compound sentence you make. The first one has been done for you as an example.

1. Do you want to wash the dishes? *or*
   Do you want to dry them?

   Do you want to wash the dishes, or do you want to dry them?

2. Ann is a carpenter. *and*
   Shelly is a banker.

3. We take our baby to Dr. Mendez. *but*
   They take their baby to Dr. Jackson.

4. I like to go sailing. *but*
   I often get seasick.

5. Where will you go on vacation? *and*
What will you do there?

____

____

6. Donnie can play the piano. *but*
He cannot read music.

____

____

7. We can eat ice cream at home. *or*
We can go out for banana splits.

____

____

____

8. Linda said she would come with us. *but*
I do not see her anywhere.

____

____

____

9. Keep the pot covered. *and*
Bring the water to a boil.

____

____

Mail Order Catalog: Part One

People often go to stores to buy food, clothes, tools, furniture and other things that they want and need. But sometimes people do their shopping by mail. People who shop by mail use a *mail order catalog* to find and order the items they want to buy. Many stores and companies print mail order catalogs so they can sell their products to people all over the country. The catalog is a book that contains all the information and order forms that a person needs to shop by mail. In this and the following chapters, you will learn how to use a mail order catalog to shop by mail.

The Index

Large mail order catalogs—those from large companies that sell many different kinds of products—have indexes to help you find what you are looking for. The *index* of a mail order catalog is a list of all the products for sale in the catalog. The listing for each item in the index tells you where in the catalog you can find buying information about that item. The information usually includes a picture and a description. You use the index of a mail order catalog to answer two questions:

1. Does the company sell the item I want to buy?
2. On what page of the catalog will I find information about the item I want to buy?

Part of a mail order catalog index is shown below.

INDEX

Auto Supplies
Batteries 890
Defrosters 935
Floor Mats 912
Lights 907
Tires 936

Bedding
Bedspreads 611
Blankets 615
Pillows 583
Sheets 374

Coats
Boys' 718
Children's 399
Girls' 414
Men's 412
Women's 123

Furniture
Benches 364
Chairs 485
Sofas 482
Tables 230

Gloves
Dress 439
Girls' 650
Ski 457
Snowmobile 457
Women's 49

In the index, find the words printed in heavy type. They are called *subject headings.* Each subject heading names a general product that the company sells—auto supplies and furniture, for example. Under the subject headings are listed the individual types of those products that the company sells. For example, under the subject heading **Auto Supplies**, you can see listings for car batteries, defrosters, floor mats, lights and tires.

Look under the subject heading **Furniture**. What types of furniture does the company sell? Print your answer on the line below.

Look again at the index. Notice the numbers printed to the right of each listing. They are page numbers. They tell you what page to turn to in the catalog to find buying information about each item. For example, suppose you want to buy a bedspread. First you find the subject heading **Bedding**. Under that subject heading you look for the kind of bedding you want—a bedspread. Next to the word *bedspreads* you see the page number 611. If you turn to page 611 in the catalog, you will find pictures, written descriptions, and the prices of all the bedspreads that are sold through the catalog.

Alphabetical Order

In the index on page 43, the subject headings are in alphabetical order. That means that they are placed in order according to the letter of the alphabet they begin with. For example, you can see that the subject headings that begin with *A* are at the beginning of the list. The subject headings that begin with *B* come next, and so on.

In the index on page 43, which subject heading is listed first, **Bedding** or **Coats**? Print your answer on the line below.

____

If the whole index were shown, it would have subject headings beginning with all the letters of the alphabet. Which of these two subject headings would be listed first in the complete index, **Sporting Goods** or **Raincoats**? Print your answer on the line below.

____

Under the subject heading, the individual products that are listed are also in alphabetical order.

Under the subject heading **Bedding**, which individual item comes first, Sheets or Pillows? Print your answer on the line below.

____

Using a Mail Order Catalog Index

You know that you use mail order catalogs to shop for products through the mail. You use the index of a catalog to find answers to the following questions:

1. Does the company sell the item I want to buy?
2. On what page will I find information about the item I want?

Here is a review of the steps you follow to use an index:

1. Find the subject heading that names the general product you are looking for. The subject headings are in alphabetical order. They are printed in heavy type.
2. Under the subject heading, find the particular item that you want. The individual items are also listed in alphabetical order.
3. Next to the particular item that you want, note the number of the page on which you can find information about that item.

Exercise 1

Here is a list of subject headings from a mail order catalog index. The subject headings name the general products that the company sells.

Jewelry
Luggage
Men's Wear
Sporting Goods

Under which of these subject headings would you look for each of the items listed below? Print the correct subject heading on the line next to each item. The first one has been done for you as an example.

1. A man's shirt Men's Wear
2. A necklace ________________
3. A baseball mitt ________________
4. A suitcase ________________
5. A necktie ________________
6. A bowling ball ________________
7. A fishing pole ________________
8. A ring ________________

INDEX

Exercise 2

Read the subject headings in the index above. You can see that they are in alphabetical order. On the lines below, print the names of the general products that the company sells. Keep them in alphabetical order. The first one has been filled in for you.

1. Rings
2. ____________________
3. ____________________
4. ____________________
5. ____________________

Exercise 3

Look again at the catalog index on page 48. Under the names of general products (the subject headings) are the names of the particular items that are sold. Next to each item is the number of the page on which you will find information about the item. Find the correct page number for each item given below. Write the page number on the line next to the item. The first one has been done for you as an example.

1. jogging shoes 496 ______
2. ski goggles ______
3. hammers ______
4. wedding rings ______
5. girls' sweaters ______
6. ballet slippers ______
7. screwdrivers ______
8. tennis shoes ______

2

Get Out!

Preview Words/*Chapter 2*

Study the words in the box. Then read the sentences below with your teacher. Look carefully at the words in boldface type.

allow	extra	neither	route
answering	forward	northern	station
counter	garage	picnic	straight
cupboard	hopefully	questions	waitress
expect	museum	restaurant	wrong

1. Highway 80 went **straight** across the state.
2. They were going across the **northern** part of Pennsylvania.
3. Rita leaned **forward** to give a thumbs-up signal.
4. They rode across the parking lot of a **restaurant**.
5. It's not much of a day for a **picnic**.
6. They walked in and sat down at the **counter**.
7. "A hamburger, please," Jeff told the **waitress**.
8. We don't **allow** dogs in here.
9. What's **wrong** with that waitress?
10. They rode past a gas **station**.
11. The van is inside the **garage**.
12. The **museum** must have opened by now.
13. They'll never **expect** us to do that.
14. "Mop didn't come with you?" she asked **hopefully**.
15. He was asking lots of **questions**.
16. Jeff was **answering** them happily.
17. The dog was in the **cupboard**.
18. **Neither** one of them said a word.
19. That will give us two **extra** days to get to San Francisco.
20. If we take the northern **route**, there will be much more to see.

Jeff and Rita pushed on across New Jersey. It was still early in the morning when Jeff pointed to another sign:

WELCOME TO PENNSYLVANIA

Another state line. Now they were in Pennsylvania! It seemed as if they were already a long way from New York City, and really on their way.

Highway 80 went straight across the northern part of Pennsylvania. The Sunday morning traffic was light, and they made good time.

They stopped in each rest area to walk a bit and give Mop a chance to run around and sniff at everything. Jeff and Rita laughed to see her running along like a little dust mop. "She has to dust off everything," Rita laughed, "just like a neat little housekeeper."

"Maybe I should use her to dust off the bike," Jeff said. "Hey, look. What is she into now? What a neat little housekeeper she is *now!*" Mop had climbed up into a trash basket and was digging around happily in the trash.

"You don't have to get into everything!" Rita told Mop and she pulled her out of the trash basket. "You're as bad as a little kid!"

"Oh don't get so upset," Jeff laughed. "You should be glad that she likes to get into things. If she didn't like it, how would we get her to California?"

"Well, just so long as she stays out of strange trucks!"

They pushed on. At lunch time they bought some food, then found a nice place by a river to eat. After they had finished eating, they just sat with their feet in the water. "What a life," Jeff said.

"Oh it's wonderful," Rita said. "This is such a great

way to travel. First you feel as if you're flying. Then you just sit in the sun. Then when you're good and ready, you fly some more."

"Well, are you good and ready?" Jeff asked.

"I sure am!" Rita said as she jumped up. "Come on, Mop, let's fly some more!"

They pushed on. That afternoon, when they crossed another state line, it was Rita who saw the sign first:

WELCOME TO OHIO

Jeff waved his arm, and the bike roared on down the road.

They camped that night near Cleveland, Ohio. The next morning, Mop woke them up by jumping around on them and licking their faces. "All right, all right," Rita said sleepily, "you can go out, but I'm going with you. We're not going to lose you again." She unzipped the tent and crawled out. Mop went running off, while Rita stood up and stretched. "Oh Jeff," she called sadly, "it's cloudy out today."

Jeff stuck his head out of the tent and looked at the sky. "Just so it doesn't rain," he said. "I think it will be all right. We can be in Chicago by the middle of the afternoon. And if it does rain, so what? We have our rain gear with us."

"You're right," Rita said. "It's just that I've never been on a bike in the rain before."

Jeff laughed. "When you go all the way across the country, you have to be ready for everything."

They pushed on across Ohio. The next state line came up quickly:

WELCOME TO INDIANA

Jeff pointed to another sign:

FOOD GAS
NEXT EXIT

Rita leaned forward to show a thumbs up signal, and Jeff took the exit. Soon they were riding across the parking lot of a restaurant. "It's not much of a day for a picnic," Jeff said, taking off his helmet and putting it on the bike. "Let's eat in this restaurant."

"Good idea," Rita said.

They walked into the restaurant and sat down at the counter. "A hamburger and a cup of coffee, please," Jeff told the waitress.

"The same for me," Rita added.

The waitress put two hamburgers on the grill. Then she put spoons and napkins on the counter in front of Rita and Jeff, and added two cups. She got the coffee pot and began to pour coffee into Rita's cup.

Just then, Mop stuck his head up out of Jeff's jacket. The waitress jumped back, and coffee ran all over the counter. "What's that?" the waitress screamed.

Jeff quickly pushed Mop's head back down inside his jacket. Rita tried to clean up the spilled coffee with her napkin. But the waitress shouted, "What *is* that? What do you have in there?"

"It's a dog," Jeff told her, unzipping his jacket and lifting Mop out. "See? Her name is Mop."

"We don't allow dogs in here!" the waitress said. "You'll have to take it outside!"

"But she's not hurting anything," Rita said. "She—"

"No dogs allowed! Now get that thing out of here!"

"Come on, Rita," Jeff said, "let's go."

They got up and walked quickly out of the restaurant. Behind them they could hear the waitress say, "Some people!"

They went back to the motorcycle and leaned up against it. "What do you want to do now?" Jeff asked.

"We'll have to tie Mop to the bike," Rita said sadly.

"Do you really want to go back in there?"

"No," Rita said, "let's go somewhere else. I don't want to see that waitress again." Mop popped her head up out of Jeff's jacket, and Rita patted her. "Poor old Mop, you weren't going to hurt that old restaurant. What's wrong with that waitress? Some people!"

Jeff and Rita got on the bike again. They rode across the parking lot and past a gas station. Then they got back on the highway and pushed on.

* * * * *

As they went by the gas station, two men were watching them. "See, I told you it was them!" Ken said. "That guy and that girl and that little dog—I told you it was them! How did they know we were here?"

"Relax, Ken," Steve said, "they *didn't* know we were here. The van is inside the garage, so they didn't see it, and they never looked at us. They just stopped to get some lunch, that's all."

"They were only in the restaurant for two minutes! They just wanted to go someplace where they could watch us!"

"Ken, you're going to drive me crazy," Steve said. He walked over and leaned against the front of the gas station. "You think that everyone is after us. Every time we stop for gas, every time we stop to eat, every person we see, you think that they're all after us."

Ken walked up and down the parking lot, then looked inside the garage. The van was parked inside with the hood up, and a man was working on the motor. "What's taking him so long?" Ken asked.

Steve laughed. "I'll bet you think he's after us too." He stood up and walked over to Ken. "Look," he said, "the guy on the bike told me that they were going to Chicago to stay for a few days. The way that bike can move, they'll be in Chicago in a few hours. They'll be at someone's house, so they won't even see us go by. We'll get going as soon as the van is fixed, and we won't stop again. We'll just keep going, right across the country to California. If they stop for a few days, they'll never catch up."

"*If* they stop," Ken growled. He turned away from Steve and started to walk around and around the parking lot. Steve just stood there watching him. He knew that Ken was thinking hard.

At last Ken said, "Look, it's Monday. The museum must have opened by now, so they must have found out that the paintings are gone. The cops must be all over

New York City looking for them. Pretty soon they're going to start checking the highways."

"So what?" Steve asked. "There are lots of highways."

"Not out west! From here to California there's just one highway. They know where we'll be, so they'll be able to pick us up anytime they want to. Or maybe they'll wait. Maybe this guy on the bike will follow us all the way to California so he can find out who we're going to sell the paintings to. Then he'll nail us all!"

"Maybe you're right," Steve said. "Well, what are we going to do about it?"

"We'll fool them! We won't go west, we'll go north. We'll go up through Iowa, then South Dakota, Wyoming and Idaho. Get it? We'll come south again through Oregon, and down into San Francisco. They'll never expect us to do that!"

"Let me think about this," Steve said. He went into the garage, got a map out of the van, and looked at it carefully. "It might work," he said. "It will take at least a day longer, but it might be worth it."

"Right," Ken said. "At least we'll get away from the two on the bike—them and their stupid little dog!"

* * * * *

Jeff and Rita got to Rita's aunt and uncle's house just as the rain began to fall. When Rita rang the doorbell, a large woman with white hair came to the door. "Hello, Aunt Meg," Rita said.

"Come in, come in!" Rita's aunt said. "Come in out of the rain! Oh I've been so worried about you! I just knew that it was going to rain. I'll bet you've both caught colds."

Rita gave her aunt a hug, then stepped back and

pushed Jeff forward. "I want you to meet my husband! This is Jeff."

"Hello, Aunt Meg," Jeff smiled.

Meg gave Jeff a quick kiss on the cheek. "I'm so glad to meet you, Jeff. I've heard so much about you from Rita's mother. I was so sorry that we couldn't get to New York City for the wedding. It must have been lovely. I'm so glad that you could come and stay with us." Meg looked around, then peeked out the window at the motorcycle parked in front of the house. "But where is Mop? She didn't come with you?" she asked hopefully.

"Oh Mop is right here," Rita said, reaching over and unzipping Jeff's jacket. Mop popped her head out and barked happily.

"Oh," Meg said.

As soon as Jeff put Mop down on the floor, she ran off, sniffing at everything. Meg watched as the little dog ran into the living room. "Will she be all right?" Meg asked.

"Oh don't worry about Mop," Rita said. "She'll be fine. She's a good dog, and she's too little to hurt anything."

Just then there was a loud crash from the living room.

Meg hurried into the living room with Rita right behind her. Jeff just stood in the hall, wishing he were somewhere else.

"My plant!" Meg shouted. "She tipped over my plant!" Mop was sniffing all around a big plant that was lying on its side on the floor.

Rita ran over to the plant and stood it up again. "Look, Aunt Meg, the plant isn't broken. Mop must have tried to get into its pot. She likes to get into things. But it's OK. I'll just clean up the dirt that spilled." She tried to pick up the dirt with her hands.

"I'll get a broom," Meg said, walking quickly out of the room.

Rita grabbed Mop and gave her a little shake. "What's the big idea?" she asked. "Are you trying to get us thrown out? We just got here!" Mop just barked and licked Rita's face.

Just then Rita's uncle got home from work. "Here's our two motorcycle bums!" he called as he burst through the door. He hugged Rita and shook Jeff's hand, grinning. "Tell me all about your trip!" Soon he was outside with Jeff, looking at the motorcycle and asking lots of questions, which Jeff was answering happily. Then he took Jeff and Rita and Mop for a drive around Chicago in his new car.

When they got home again, supper was ready. Rita and Jeff found that they were very hungry. "It's nice to eat at a table again!" Rita said.

"Oh dear, you poor children!" Meg said. "Was your trip really that bad?"

"Oh no, Aunt Meg, it wasn't bad at all, it was fun!" Rita said quickly. "I like camping, and I love riding the motorcycle. It's just like flying!"

"Well you must call your mother right after supper," Meg said. "She called here last night to find out if we had heard from you. She's worried sick about you!"

"Yes, Aunt Meg, I'll call her."

"And don't you think you should give up this trip?" Meg went on. "Why don't you let us put you on a plane to San Francisco? It would be so much safer!"

"Now, Meg," Rita's uncle broke in, "let them do what they want. I'm sure they have planned it well. They got here, didn't they? Now, Jeff, we're all going to a baseball game tonight. I've got four tickets."

"That sounds great!" Jeff said.

When they finished supper, Jeff and Rita's uncle were still talking about baseball. Rita went off to call her mother.

"Oh I'm so glad you called!" her mother said as soon as she picked up the phone. "I've been so upset! Wait until you hear—the museum was robbed over the weekend!"

"Robbed!"

"Yes, robbed!" Rita's mother went on. "This morning when we opened up we found out that twenty paintings had been stolen!"

"Wow, that's a lot!" Rita said.

"The police were here all day," Rita's mother said. "They said that the robbers must have been here for a long time. The robbers even took the time to wrap the paintings! They left some brown paper and rope on the floor, out in the hallway. But the police don't have any idea who it was. The paintings are just gone!"

"Now, now, Mom, don't worry," Rita said. "The police will find them. They can't have gone very far. Don't worry . . ."

While Rita was on the phone, her aunt was washing the supper dishes. Then she went upstairs to get ready for the baseball game. She didn't see Mop following her up the stairs.

Meg went into her bedroom, opened the closet door, got out a box, and opened it. Her new wig . . . Maybe she would wear her new wig to the baseball game.

She put the box down on the bed and went into the bathroom to wash up. Mop came in from the hallway and started to sniff around the bedroom. Then she spotted the wig box. She jumped up on the bed and sniffed at the wig. It would make such a nice, soft bed for a dog. She got into the box, curled up on the wig, and went to sleep.

Meg came back into the bedroom and changed into a clean dress. Then she reached into the wig box, picked up the soft lump of hair, and put it on her head.

Mop barked.

Meg screamed and fell across the bed. Downstairs, Rita's uncle jumped to his feet and called, "Meg, what happened?" He ran up the stairs with Rita and Jeff right behind him.

"That dog! That awful little dog! I thought . . . I put . . . My wig!" Meg screamed.

"Now, now, Meg," Rita's uncle said, "take it easy. The dog didn't hurt your wig. It's right here in the box."

"No, no, the *dog* was in the box! I thought it was my wig, and I put it on my head!"

"You put the dog on your head?" Rita's uncle started to laugh. "I always thought that wig looked like a dog!" He laughed harder and harder, and Jeff had to put his hand over his mouth so that he wouldn't laugh too. Even Rita started to smile.

"Well a lot of help *you* are!" Meg said. "You'd better get going or you'll be late for your baseball game. I'm not going. I'm going to lie down for a while!"

"Oh, Meg, don't . . ." Rita's uncle started to say.

"Oh, Aunt Meg, I'm sorry . . ." Rita began.

"Go on, all of you! And lock that dog in the garage while you're gone!" Meg shouted, pushing them out of the room and closing the door.

"What are we going to do?" Rita asked her uncle.

"Oh, she'll be all right. Come on, we'll be late for that game." He led the way down the stairs, still laughing.

"By the way, Rita," Jeff said, "how is your mother? What did she say when you called her?"

"Oh, something happened at the museum where she works. Some pictures were stolen, and she was all upset."

"Sounds like your mother," Jeff said.

"You can tell that she and Meg are sisters," Rita's uncle said. "Let's go to that game."

* * * * *

The next morning, when Jeff and Rita came down to breakfast, Mop followed them down the stairs. She ran around the living room barking, then ran into the kitchen.

A moment later they heard a scream from the kitchen. Rita's uncle jumped up from the table and called, "Meg, are you all right?" Rita's aunt came through the kitchen door. Her face was pale, and she was shaking. "What happened?" Rita's uncle asked.

"The dog . . . The dog was in the cupboard . . . She

must have got in while my back was turned. Then when I bent down to get a pot out of the cupboard, she jumped out at me! She jumped out right in my face!"

"Now, now, it's all right," Rita's uncle said. "I'm sure she didn't mean to scare you."

"I'll tie her up outside," Jeff said quickly. "Come on, Mop, let's go."

A few minutes later, they all sat down to eat breakfast. Rita could see Mop out the window. The little dog was pulling on the rope and barking loudly.

"Now, children," Rita's aunt was saying, "I really feel that you should stop this crazy trip. You just can't go across the country on a motorcycle."

"But, Aunt Meg—" Rita started to say.

"But nothing! You can stay right here in Chicago and have your honeymoon with us, and next week we'll put you on a plane."

"But, Aunt Meg—"

"Think how much better your mother will feel. You can take that nasty little dog on the plane with you."

"But, Aunt Meg—"

"But really," Meg went right on, "I don't see why you want to keep that dog. If you took her down to the dog pound, they would find her a new home or just put her away."

"Oh, Aunt Meg." Rita put her face in her hands. She could hear Mop outside, barking and barking.

After breakfast, as Rita helped her aunt clear the table, neither one of them said a word. Then Rita went into the living room looking for Jeff. He was sitting on the floor with a big map spread out in front of him. "What are you doing?" Rita asked.

Jeff looked up at her and said, "Smile, darling, I've got it all worked out."

"What?"

"Well we can't stay here, not with your dog—and my bike. Right?"

Rita sat down on the floor next to him. "Right," she said sadly.

"We'll get on the road again today," Jeff said, "right after lunch. That will give us two extra days to get to San Francisco, so we can do some extra riding. Look at the map. We were going to go this way, due west, right across the country. It's all flat out there, with nothing to look at but corn."

"Well . . ."

"So we can go up this way," Jeff went on, pointing to the map as he spoke. "We'll head north, through nothern Iowa, then go into South Dakota, then Wyoming, then Idaho. See? Then we'll go through Oregon and take some time to see the big redwood trees. Then south into San Francisco, and we'll be in our new home. How about it? If we take the northern route there will be lots more to see!"

Rita looked toward the kitchen. "I'll have to tell my aunt . . ."

"Just tell her we had to change our plans. I think she'll be glad to get rid of us!" Four hours later they were on the road.

Half a day behind the van.

Comprehension Questions/Chapter 2

Directions. Answer these questions about the chapter you have just read. Put an *x* in the box beside the best answer to each question.

1. (C) Which of the following happened first?

☐ a. The waitress spilled the coffee on the counter.
☐ b. Mop popped out of Jeff's jacket.
☐ c. The waitress put spoons and cups down on the counter.
☐ d. The waitress asked, "What *is* that?"

2. (D) Why did Rita and Jeff leave the restaurant?

☐ a. They were after the men in the van.
☐ b. They didn't like the food.
☐ c. They didn't want to eat in a place where they couldn't bring Mop.
☐ d. They thought it would be more fun to have a picnic.

3. (B) Why did the two men stop in Indiana?

☐ a. They wanted to get something to eat.
☐ b. They had to get their van fixed.
☐ c. They wanted to sell the paintings to a museum.
☐ d. They knew that Jeff and Rita were there.

4. (A) Ken said, "Maybe this guy on the bike will follow us all the way to California so he can find out who we're going to sell the paintings to. Then *he'll nail us all!*" What does this mean?

- ☐ a. He'll try to build something for us.
- ☐ b. He'll hit all of us with his hands.
- ☐ c. He'll try to buy all the paintings.
- ☐ d. He'll put all of us in jail.

5. (E) What is the main thing the two men were afraid of?

- ☐ a. Having the van break down again
- ☐ b. Having to stay with Rita's aunt
- ☐ c. Getting caught with the stolen paintings
- ☐ d. Getting lost on the way to California

6. (C) What was the first thing Mop did when she got to Aunt Meg's house?

- ☐ a. She got into the wig box.
- ☐ b. She went for a ride in a car.
- ☐ c. She tipped over a plant.
- ☐ d. She ran into the kitchen.

7. (B) What did Mop do to scare Meg in the kitchen?

- ☐ a. She jumped on the stove.
- ☐ b. She jumped out of a cupboard.
- ☐ c. She barked in back of her.
- ☐ d. She jumped out of a pan.

8. (A) Rita's aunt said that the dog pound would find a new home for Mop or *put her away*. What does this mean?

- ☐ a. Keep her locked up
- ☐ b. Give her back to Rita
- ☐ c. Put her on a plane
- ☐ d. Kill her

9. (D) Why did Jeff and Rita leave Chicago two days early?

- ☐ a. They couldn't get along with Rita's aunt.
- ☐ b. They had no place to stay.
- ☐ c. They were afraid that they wouldn't get to San Francisco in time.
- ☐ d. They wanted to follow the men in the van.

10. (E) What is the main thing that you should know at the end of this part of the story?

- ☐ a. Jeff and Rita will be taking the same road as the van after all.
- ☐ b. Jeff and Rita will be taking a plane to San Francisco.
- ☐ c. The men in the van will turn around and go back to New York City.
- ☐ d. The men in the van will stay in Chicago.

Skills Used to Answer Questions

A. Recognizing Words in Context
B. Recalling Facts
C. Keeping Events in Order
D. Making Inferences
E. Understanding Main Ideas

Commas in a List of Items

You know that a comma is a punctuation mark that tells you to pause in a sentence. In the last lesson you learned that a comma goes before the connecting word in a compound sentence. Now you will learn about another way that commas are used. Read the sentence below.

> Pearl planted roses, tulips, pansies, and lilies in her garden.

The sentence gives you a *list* of the flowers that Pearl planted in her garden. Notice the commas in the sentence. You need commas in a sentence when you have a *list of three or more items.* A comma belongs after each item in the list except the very last item. Each comma tells you to pause before going on to the next word in the sentence. Look at the sentence below.

> Bess will need new shoes, a new hat, and a new dress for the wedding.

The sentence gives a list of clothes that Bess will need. You can see that a comma is placed after each item of clothing except the last. What do the commas tell you to do?

Exercise 1

The sentences below have no commas. Rewrite each sentence on the line provided, placing a comma after each item in a list of three or more items. Remember that you should not put a comma after the very last item in the list. The first one has been done for you as an example.

1. Our family has one dog two cats three birds and two turtles.

   Our family has one dog, two cats, three birds, and two turtles.

2. Kate gave me a rake a spade and a hoe.

   ____

   ____

3. Pick up eggs oranges bread and milk at the supermarket.

   ____

   ____

4. You can get books records and tapes at our library.

   ____

   ____

5. Tom was wearing a gray suit a light blue shirt and a blue-striped tie.

____

____

____

6. We packed toothbrushes toothpaste soap shampoo and razors in our suitcases.

____

____

____

Commas in a List of Actions

You know that you must use a comma after each item in a list of three or more items. The items in the sentences you have read so far are *things,* such as flowers or pieces of clothing. But the items in a list may also be *actions,* such as riding a bike or taking a trip. Look at the sentences below.

> Next year I want to visit Italy, hike in the Alps, and see a bullfight in Spain.
>
> The winner of the contest must swim three miles, bike thirty miles, and run twenty-six miles.

When you are given a list of three or more actions, you must put a comma after each action except the last one. Remember that the commas tell you to pause slightly.

Exercise 2

Each sentence below contains a list of three or more items. Some of the items are things. Some of the items are actions. The sentences have been written without commas. Print each sentence on the lines provided, putting a comma after each item in the list except the last item. The first sentence has been done for you as an example.

1. Today I must buy food bake a cake and cook dinner.

   Today I must buy food, bake a cake, and cook dinner.

2. Carmen got in the car put on her seatbelt started the engine and drove down the street.

3. I need an oil pan a wrench an oil filter and three cans of oil to change the oil in my car.

4. Please wash the dishes wipe off the table and sweep the floor.

____

____

____

5. Tomorrow I am leaving work early catching the 3:00 train and going to Dallas.

____

____

____

6. Mary Lou put stars angels and colored lights on her Christmas tree.

____

____

____

7. A waitress must take the order serve the food remove the dishes and give the bill to the customer.

____

____

____

Mail Order Catalog: Part Two

You know that you use mail order catalogs to shop for products through the mail. You also know how to use the index of a catalog to find the items you are looking for in the catalog.

For each item sold in the catalog, there is a written description. The description of an item in a mail order catalog is called an *entry*. Below is a catalog entry for an all-weather coat. Look at the entry.

> **B. All-Weather Coat.** Of woven cotton and polyester. Waterproof. Zip-out lining. Removable hood. Tie belt. Machine washable.
> Colors: 44 tan; 52 red; 38 navy blue
> Women's sizes: 6, 8, 10, 12, 14, 16
> Z-261 Delivery weight 3.2 lbs. $69.00

The entry for the all-weather coat gives you the following information:

1. The letter *B* tells you that the picture labeled "B" on this page of the catalog is a picture of the coat described in this entry.
2. The heading "All-Weather Coat" tells you what the product is.
3. The words "Of woven cotton and polyester. Waterproof. Zip-out lining. Removable hood. Tie belt. Machine washable" tell about the fabric and special features of the coat.
4. You are told that the coat comes in three colors: tan, red and navy blue. In this entry, you are also given color code numbers: 44 for tan, 52 for red, and 38 for navy blue. Some catalogs do not have code numbers

for colors. Entries in those catalogs list colors by name only.

5. You are told that the coat comes in women's sizes 6, 8, 10, 12, 14, and 16.
6. You are given a *catalog number* for the coat. Each item in the catalog has its own special number. The catalog number is used to identify the item. The catalog number for the all-weather coat is Z-261. This catalog number has a letter (Z) before the number. Some catalog numbers have no letter.
7. You are told that the coat weighs 3.2 pounds (lbs.).
8. You are told that the coat costs $69.00.

In large mail order catalogs, you will find entries for many kinds of products, including such things as tools, furniture and appliances. Entries for those kinds of products look very much like entries for clothing. They give you a lot of the same information, such as the color, catalog number, delivery weight, and price. But the description of a tool or appliance will not give you a choice of sizes. It will give you special information about how the product works. A catalog entry for a toaster is shown below.

> **D. 2-Slice Toaster.** Variable thermostat for toast settings. Steel body and crumb tray. Measures 8 by 4 by 7 inches high. Single control. 1050 watts.
> Color code and name: 145 lemon
> 5784 Delivery weight 4.8 lbs. $17.99

The catalog entry gives you the toaster's color—lemon. The entry also tells you the weight of the toaster (4.8 lbs.), its catalog number (5784), and its price ($17.99). The special information in the toaster entry tells you how the toaster works. For example, the words "Variable thermostat for toast settings" tell you that you can set the toaster to cook light, dark or medium toast. You are also given electrical information about the toaster's controls (Single control) and power (1050 watts).

You read catalog entries to get information about the products you are interested in buying. From that information, you decide whether or not to buy the product.

Reading a Catalog Entry

You know that mail order catalog entries describe the items offered for sale in the catalog. An entry gives you information that helps you decide if you want to buy the item.

Exercise

Read the catalog entries that follow. Use the information in each entry to answer the questions below it. Print your answers on the lines provided. The first one has been done for you as an example.

1. **E. Travel Bag.** Of rayon canvas with vinyl trim. Shoulder strap. Front pocket with zipper. Toiletry kit. Measures 21 by 18 by 9 inches deep.
Colors: 53 brown; 82 black.
Z-649 Delivery weight 7.7 lbs. $49.75

a. Which picture on the page is a picture of the travel bag? E

b. What fabric is the bag made of?

rayon canvas with vinyl trim

c. In what colors can you buy the bag?

brown and black

d. What is the color code number for the bag? 82

e. What is the catalog number for black? Z-649

f. How much does the travel bag weigh? 7.7 lbs.

g. How much does the travel bag cost? $49.75

2. **G. Men's Sweatshorts.** Of rayon-cotton blend. Elastic waist. Back pocket. Machine wash warm.
Sizes: Small, Medium, Large
Colors: gray, blue
6930 Delivery weight 1 lb. $9.00

a. Which picture on the page is a picture of the shorts?

____

b. What fabric are the shorts made of?

____

c. How should you wash the shorts?

____

d. In what sizes can you buy the shorts?

____

e. What is the catalog number for the shorts?

____

f. How much do the shorts weigh? ______________

g. How much do the shorts cost? ______________

3. **A. 20-Inch, 3-Speed Portable Fan.** Variable thermostat to set temperature. Five plastic blades. Tan enamel finish on steel. Convenient carrying handle. 21 by 6 by 22 inches high. 180 watts.
R-785 Delivery weight 16.5 lbs. $29.99

a. Which picture on the page is a picture of the fan?

____

b. How much electric power does the fan use?

____

c. What is the catalog number for the fan? _______

d. How much does the fan weigh? _______________

e. How much does the fan cost? _______________

4. **C. Lightweight Folding Stroller.** Painted vinyl seat padded with nylon fabric. Removable canopy. Adjustable safety strap. Steel frame. Friction brake. Plastic handles.
343 Delivery weight 5 lbs. $35.00

a. Which picture on the page is a picture of the stroller? _______________

b. What material is the stroller's frame made of?

____

c. What type of brake does the stroller have?

____

d. What is the catalog number for the stroller?

____

e. How much does the stroller weigh? __________

f. How much does the stroller cost? __________

3

The Badlands

Preview Words/Chapter 3

Study the words in the box. Then read the sentences below with your teacher. Look carefully at the words in boldface type.

angrily	crumbled	millions	thirsty
breath	echo	monument	trailers
carved	edges	ravine	twisted
colored	enough	shadow	unrolling
covered	giant	shoulders	western

1. The land was flat, **covered** with tall grass.
2. The rocks were cut by deep **ravines**.
3. The ravines **twisted** this way and that.
4. The cut **edges** of the ravine showed stripes of color.
5. The strange **colored** rocks went on and on.
6. There are badlands in other **western** states.
7. The rocks were worn down over **millions** of years.
8. The signs told about how the wind and water had **carved** the rocks.
9. Her voice came back from the cliffs in an **echo**.
10. The rock just **crumbled** under her hands and feet.
11. She was very hot and **thirsty**.
12. She held her **breath** and listened.
13. Rita was **unrolling** the fishing line as she walked.
14. There was a black **shadow** under the rock.
15. Jeff said **angrily**, "I'm not mad, I'm just hot!"
16. There were other people on the road, mostly families in cars with **trailers**.
17. Soon they were in the parking lot of the Mount Rushmore **Monument**.
18. There was Mount Rushmore—four **giant** heads looking down at them.
19. Have you seen **enough** of Mount Rushmore?
20. He shrugged his **shoulders** and said, "Who cares?"

Jeff and Rita rode through Illinois, then cut through Iowa. In two days they were roaring across South Dakota.

The land was flat, covered with tall grass as far as they could see. The highway was flat and open, and the miles went by quickly.

They were making good time, but Rita began to wish that they could stop for a while. If only there was something to stop and look at! Mile after mile, the grassland rushed by. Grass, grass, grass—there seemed to be nothing in South Dakota but grass! Back in Chicago, Jeff had seemed so sure that there would be more to see if they went farther north. Well here they were, farther north, and there was nothing to look at but grass.

Suddenly she saw a highway sign:

BADLANDS

NEXT EXIT

Badlands? What on earth could that mean? Well, it would be something to look at. She bumped Jeff on the back and was about to point out the sign to him when she saw that he was already turning off the highway.

They rode down a side road for a few miles. Rita looked all around, with her eyes and mouth open wide. The land around them had suddenly become so strange! What kind of place was this? It was very dry, and the grasslands were gone. There was nothing but rocks. The rocks were cut by deep ravines that twisted this way and that. The sides of the ravines were very steep, and they showed stripes of many colors—pink, brown, white, more pink. Rita had never seen anything like it before.

As they came over a hill, Rita gasped: the strange rocks went on and on as far as they could see. The ravines, the colored rocks, on and on.

Jeff pulled into a parking lot. As they swung off the bike and took off their helmets, they could feel that the air was hot and dry. "Where are we?" Rita asked. "What *is* this place?"

"It's called the Badlands," Jeff said. "I've read about it, and I thought it might be fun to have a look at it. There are badlands in other states in the western part of the country, too. The rocks were cut by wind and water, a long, long time ago. They were worn down into ravines slowly, over millions of years. Now the water is gone and it's just dry, dry, dry."

"Yes, I can see that—nothing can grow here." Rita turned around slowly. "*Look* at this place! What a great place to play hide-and-seek!"

"You're right about that," Jeff laughed. "In the old days, a hundred years ago, robbers used to hide in the badlands. They could hide here for as long as they wanted, and no one could ever find them."

He unzipped his jacket and put Mop down. Mop shook herself for a moment, then ran around the bike, sniffing at the ground. "Don't go too far, Mop," Jeff called after her. "We don't want to lose you here!"

Rita pulled off her jacket and threw it over the bike. She pushed her hair back from her face. "It sure is hot," she said.

"Yes, the sun is very strong." Jeff walked slowly across the parking lot, humming to himself.

"Look, Jeff," Rita called, "there's a path. Let's look around a little."

"OK, but we have to be careful. We must not get lost. Remember those robbers. The good guys never found them."

Rita laughed. "Well, we'll just go a little way."

As they began to follow the path into a ravine, they saw a sign:

DANGER

The Badlands are full of danger.
Do not go into the Badlands without water.

"Boy, they really mean it!" Rita said.

As they walked on down the path, Rita looked back and saw that the parking lot was already out of sight. All around them were those strange striped rocks.

They walked on for a few more minutes, with Mop running along by their feet. It felt good to walk after riding for so long.

The path twisted in and out of the main ravine, and smaller ravines went off on all sides. It was such a strange place—a whole new world. There were little signs along the path that told about the rocks and how the wind and water had carved them. Rita stopped to read each sign as she came to it, so that she could find out more about this strange place.

Suddenly she heard a noise behind her. Mop was running down a little ravine that went off to one side of the path. The little ravine twisted away to the right, and in a moment Mop was out of sight. "Mop, come back!" Rita called. "Mop!" her voice came back from the cliffs all around her. "Mop . . . Mop . . . Mop . . ." the echo said.

"I'll get her!" Jeff said. He ran off down the little ravine shouting, "Mop, get back here!"

"Jeff, wait!" Rita called, but he didn't hear her. In a moment he was gone too.

Rita stood still. She could hear Jeff calling to Mop, but she couldn't tell where his voice was coming from. The echo was everywhere at once. She stepped off the path and slowly followed the little ravine. She walked around the first bend, but she couldn't see Jeff. She followed the little ravine as it twisted off to the left. Suddenly it opened into a bigger ravine. Everywhere she looked there were more openings. Jeff and Mop could have gone into any one of them.

"Jeff! Jeff!" she called. Then she held her breath and listened. She could hear nothing but the wind stirring the dust around her feet.

If she could get up higher, maybe she could see them. She tried to climb up the side of the ravine to see if she could look down into the other ravines from the top. But the rock just crumbled under her hands and feet, and she fell back down to the bottom. As she jumped up again, she could feel fear rising in her. She wanted to run around and scream, but she wouldn't let herself do it. She made herself sit down and think.

She sat on a rock and leaned back against the side of the ravine, but the rocks were so hot from the sun that

she had to sit up again. She looked around. The sun was beating down into the ravine and shining off the rocks so brightly that it hurt her eyes.

And it was hot.

Suddenly Rita thought about how dry it was all around her. She was very hot and thirsty, and she didn't have any water with her. What about Jeff? He had been running, so he must really need some water by now. Rita jumped up. She had to find him. She had to! But how? She sat down again and waited.

Suddenly she heard a little noise behind her, coming closer and closer, and Mop popped out of a ravine by her side. "Mop!" Rita shouted, grabbing the little dog and hugging her. "Is Jeff coming? Where is he?" She held her breath and listened. There was no sound.

She had to find Jeff, and soon. Mop could find him, but first she had to think of a way so that she wouldn't get lost too. She walked back up the ravine to the path, holding Mop in her arms. She followed the path back to the parking lot, where the bike stood looking as if nothing had happened. Rita got out the rope and tied Mop to the bike, then looked in the bike's saddlebags for the jug of water that they kept for Mop. She took a sip. It was warm, but it tasted so good!

She went on looking through the saddlebags. She didn't really know what she was looking for, but it gave her something to do while she tried to think of how to find Jeff. She dug down to the very bottom of the saddlebags and found a lot of old tools and rags that Jeff never took out. Suddenly she found something: a roll of fishing line. Jeff must have gone fishing sometime. It was a big roll, and it was just what she needed.

She tied one end of the fishing line to the bike, then picked up the water jug. She took Mop's rope and pulled

Mop back down the path until she found the little ravine that Mop and Jeff had gone down. "Come on, Mop, find Jeff!" she said.

Mop ran down the ravine, pulling against the rope. Rita ran after her, unrolling the fishing line as she went along. They went down one ravine and into another, twisting and turning, to the left and the right and back again. But still Mop pulled against the rope.

Rita had to make Mop stop for a moment. She was so tired, and the sun was so hot. She felt sick and dizzy. A person could die out here and just dry up, and no one would ever find him.

She had to find Jeff! Quickly she took a sip of water from the jug and poured some into her hand for Mop. Then she said, "Go on, Mop, find Jeff."

Mop ran on down another ravine that looked just like all the others. Did Mop really know where she was going? Then, as they went around another bend, Mop started to bark. Rita blinked her eyes in the bright sun. Mop was barking at a rock that stuck out from the wall of the ravine. There was a shadow under the rock, black against the bright sunlight. Rita blinked her eyes again. Something was moving under the rock—something big. It was coming out. It was Jeff.

Jeff crawled out from under the rock and stood up slowly, holding onto the side of the ravine. He looked as if he felt dizzy. "Had to find some shade . . ." he said slowly. "Had to get out of the sun . . ."

Rita ran to him and threw her arms around him. "Oh, Jeff," she said, "I didn't know where you were! Oh, darling, I was so worried!"

Jeff pushed her away and pointed at the water jug. "Water!" he gasped.

"Oh yes, I'm sorry," Rita said as she gave him the

water jug. He took a big sip, and another, and another. At last he gave the jug back to Rita, and she took a sip too.

Mop was running around their feet, barking happily. Her barking echoed up and down the ravine. "Shut up!" Jeff yelled at her.

"Now, Jeff," Rita said, "she's just glad to see you. And if it hadn't been for Mop I never would have found you!"

"If it hadn't been for Mop I never would have got lost!" Jeff growled. "Now how are we going to get out of here?"

"We just follow this," Rita said, showing Jeff the fishing line. "The other end is tied to the bike."

"Well aren't you smart!" Jeff snapped. He walked quickly away, following the fishing line.

Rita hurried after him, pulling Mop along behind her. "Please, Jeff, don't be mad," she called.

Jeff stopped and said angrily, "I'm not mad, I'm just hot!" But he waited for her, and they all walked back to the bike together, rolling up the fishing line as they went.

It seemed so easy, now that they knew the way, and soon they were back at the parking lot. Rita turned around slowly, looking at the colored rocks all around them. "This is quite a place," she said, "and the rocks are really pretty, but I've seen all I need to see. I just want to get out of here."

"I know what you mean," Jeff said, grabbing for his helmet and his jacket. "Come here, you good-for-nothing dog!" he said as he stuffed Mop down inside his jacket. Rita was already on the bike, and Jeff jumped on and started it up. "Next stop Mount Rushmore!" he shouted.

"I hope they sell ice cream there," Rita said. "I think I could eat a ton of it right now."

"Let's go look," Jeff said. "I could eat two tons of it

myself." The bike roared out of the badlands parking lot.

* * * * *

They left the Badlands behind them. Soon they were riding through pine woods, so lovely after the dry rocks of the Badlands—and so much cooler. They passed hills and lakes. Now the Badlands seemed like just a bad dream. Rita leaned back on the sissy bar and sang a little song to herself.

As the bike roared along the highway to Mount Rushmore, they saw lots of other people on the road, mostly big vans or families in cars with trailers. The bike zipped around them easily, and soon Rita and Jeff were in the parking lot of the Mount Rushmore Monument.

As they walked toward the monument, they passed cars from every state in the United States. "The whole country is here!" Rita said.

"Look!" Jeff said, pointing up. There in front of them was Mount Rushmore—four giant heads looking down at them.

"It's so *big!*" Rita gasped.

"Well it *is* a whole mountain," Jeff said.

They got some ice cream at an ice cream stand and sat on a bench in the shade and looked up at the giant faces while they ate. Then they got some more ice cream and sat down again to eat it. Then they got some *more* ice cream.

"Well have you seen enough of Mount Rushmore?" Jeff asked. "We might as well find a campground."

"OK. Just let me get a postcard for my mother," Rita said. "I think Mount Rushmore would be a good card to send to her."

"You aren't going to tell her all about the Badlands?" Jeff asked. "You aren't going to tell her about

how you and your dog made a fool out of your new husband?"

"Now, now, darling, cheer up," Rita told him. "Have some more ice cream or something. Besides, my mother has enough to worry about," she added as she bought the postcard. She wrote a quick note to her mother, then put a stamp on the postcard and dropped it into a mailbox.

They walked back through the parking lot to the bike, with Mop running along behind them. "I wonder how my mother is doing," Rita said. "I wonder if things are OK at the museum where she works. Do you think they ever found those robbers and got those paintings back?"

Jeff just shrugged his shoulders and said, "Who cares? New York seems very far away. It doesn't have anything to do with us anymore."

They got on the bike and headed for the highway. Soon they were roaring down the road toward Wyoming. The new Yamaha bike was holding up very well, and they were making good time.

They were making such good time that they had almost caught up with the van.

Comprehension Questions/*Chapter 3*

Directions. Answer these questions about the chapter you have just read. Put an *x* in the box beside the best answer to each question.

1. (A) As they rode across South Dakota, Jeff and Rita were *making good time.* What does this mean?

- ☐ a. They were having fun.
- ☐ b. They were able to travel quickly.
- ☐ c. They were talking about old times.
- ☐ d. They were having a good honeymoon.

2. (B) What carved out the rocks in the Badlands?

- ☐ a. People from long ago
- ☐ b. Frost action
- ☐ c. Wind and water
- ☐ d. The hot sun

3. (D) How did the Badlands get its name?

- ☐ a. Robbers and other bad people were sent there.
- ☐ b. It was a very bad place for a campground.
- ☐ c. The water there was bad to drink.
- ☐ d. It was full of danger and nothing could grow there.

4. (C) Which of these things happened first?

- ☐ a. Jeff ran after Mop.
- ☐ b. Mop ran away down the ravine.
- ☐ c. Mop ran up behind Rita.
- ☐ d. Rita sat down to think.

5. (E) What did Jeff need the most in the Badlands?

- ☐ a. Water and shade
- ☐ b. Something to eat
- ☐ c. Ice cream
- ☐ d. Gas and oil

6. (D) Why was Jeff angry when Rita found him?

- ☐ a. He felt as if he hadn't been very smart.
- ☐ b. He was hoping that Rita wouldn't find him.
- ☐ c. He thought that Rita had taken too long.
- ☐ d. He thought that Rita was making fun of him.

7. (C) What happened next after Rita found Jeff?

- ☐ a. They went back to the parking lot.
- ☐ b. Rita got a postcard for her mother.
- ☐ c. Jeff yelled at Mop to stop barking.
- ☐ d. Rita gave Jeff the jug of water.

8. (B) After Rita found Jeff, how did they find their way back to the parking lot?

- ☐ a. By following Mop
- ☐ b. By following a fishing line
- ☐ c. By listening for the sound of the motorcycle's motor
- ☐ d. By shouting for help

9. (A) By the time they got to Mount Rushmore, the Badlands *seemed like just a bad dream.* What does this mean?

- ☐ a. Jeff and Rita thought they had been asleep.
- ☐ b. Jeff and Rita were afraid of what had happened.
- ☐ c. Jeff and Rita felt that the whole trip was turning out to be terrible.
- ☐ d. Jeff and Rita felt as if it had never really happened.

10. (E) What is the most important thing that happened in this chapter?

- ☐ a. Jeff got lost in the Badlands.
- ☐ b. Mop ran off into the Badlands.
- ☐ c. Rita and Jeff ate a lot of ice cream at Mount Rushmore.
- ☐ d. Jeff and Rita took a walk in the Badlands.

Skills Used to Answer Questions

A. Recognizing Words in Context
B. Recalling Facts
C. Keeping Events in Order
D. Making Inferences
E. Understanding Main Ideas

Commas with Quotations

You know that a comma is a punctuation mark that tells you where to pause in a sentence. In the first two lessons, you learned how to use commas in compound sentences and in sentences that have lists of items. Now you will learn another way to use commas in sentences. Read the sentences below.

> "I mailed Carla's birthday present yesterday," said Jim.
>
> Maria asked, "Will you fly to San Francisco next week?"

In these sentences, you are given the exact words that Jim and Maria used. The exact words used by a speaker are called a *quotation*. The *quotation marks* (" ") in each sentence tell you that you are reading the speaker's exact words.

Notice that each sentence with a quotation contains a comma. The comma sets the quotation off from the rest of the sentence. The comma comes between the speaker's exact words (in quotation marks) and the rest of the sentence. Sometimes the quotation is given at the beginning of the sentence:

> "I found your house very quickly," said Peter.

When the quotation comes at the beginning of the sentence, the comma is placed at the end of the quotation, inside the quotation marks. The comma tells you to pause before going on to the rest of the sentence.

Sometimes the quotation is given at the end of the sentence:

Betty said, "Thank you for your help."

When the quotation comes at the end of the sentence, the comma is placed right after the last word in the sentence that comes before the quotation.

Exercise 1

The following sentences give you the speaker's exact words in quotation marks. The sentences have been written without commas. Print the sentences on the lines provided, putting in commas where they are needed. Remember that you use a comma to set a quotation off from the rest of the sentence. The first sentence has been done for you as an example.

1. "I already put gas in the car" said Roberta.

   "I already put gas in the car,"
   said Roberta.

2. Steve said "You can stay at our house."

   ____
   ____

3. "My son is getting a dog for his birthday" said Danny.

   ____
   ____

4. “I made these curtains myself” said Mike.

____

____

5. Jesse said “We will pick you up at 8:30 in the morning.”

____

____

6. “I will check the football standings in the paper” said Anita.

____

____

7. Ralph asked “Is the mall open on Sundays?”

____

____

8. Paul said “I never learned to swim.”

____

____

9. “Be careful crossing the street” Lucia said.

____

____

Making Your Own Sentences with Quotations

If you want to write a sentence that tells exactly what a person said, you need to know who the speaker was and what his or her words were. Your sentence will contain a quotation. Look at the example below.

Exact words spoken: My favorite music is jazz
Speaker: Ted

Two ways of writing this in a sentence are:

"My favorite music is jazz," Ted said.
Ted said, "My favorite music is jazz."

In the first sentence, the quotation comes at the beginning of the sentence. Notice the comma at the end of the quotation. It is at the very end of the quotation, inside the quotation marks. In the second sentence, the quotation comes at the end of the sentence. The comma is placed after the last word before the quotation begins. The comma tells you to pause slightly.

Below is another example. Find the comma in each of the two sentences with quotations.

Exact words spoken: I worked on my car all day
Speaker: Louise

"I worked on my car all day," said Louise.
Louise said, "I worked on my car all day."

When you make your own sentences with quotations, you must put a comma between the quotation and the rest of the sentence. What does the comma tell you to do?

Exercise 2

In each question below you are given the name of a speaker and the speaker's exact words. Use that information to make two sentences with quotations. Print the two sentences on the lines provided. On the top lines, print a sentence with the quotation at the beginning of the sentence. On the bottom lines, print a sentence with the quotation at the end of the sentence. Be sure to put a comma between the quotation and the rest of the sentence. The first one has been done for you as an example.

1. "I want some ice cream."
   The speaker is Brenda.

   "I want some ice cream," said Brenda.

   Brenda said, "I want some ice cream."

2. "Turn off the TV."
   The speaker is Bill.

3. "Our house was just painted."
The speaker is Deanna.

4. "You can take the eight o'clock bus."
The speaker is Lisa.

5. "Have some more salad."
The speaker is David.

6. "I earned a lot of money last year."
The speaker is Christina.

Mail Order Forms

You know that a mail order catalog entry describes an item that you can buy through the mail. The information in the entry helps you decide if you want to buy the item. If you do want to buy the item, you must order it from the company that prints the catalog.

To order an item through the mail, you must first fill out the order form in the catalog. An order form has three sections:

1. The first section asks for information about you—your name, address and phone number.
2. The second section asks for information about the item you are buying—name, catalog number, size, color, price and weight.
3. The third section asks you to figure out and fill in the total cost of your order.

In this chapter you will learn how to fill in shopper information and item information.

Shopper Information

The first section of the order form asks you to print your name, address and telephone number. It looks like this:

AREA CODE ( ) HOME PHONE NUMBER	
NAME (first, middle initial, last)	
ADDRESS	
CITY/STATE	ZIP CODE

Item Information

The second section of the order form asks for information about the items you are ordering. You can find the information you need in the catalog entry that describes the item. For example, suppose you want to buy a pink twin-size bedspread. The bedspread is described in the entry below, which was copied from page 95 of the catalog.

> **C. Pinstripe Bedspread.** Cotton and polyester blend. Rounded bottom corners. White ruffles. Machine wash.
> Colors: 7 pink; 3 sky blue; 17 apple green
> Twin (76 by 110 inches)
> Z-729-21 Delivery weight 4.3 lbs. $25.99
> Full (90 by 110 inches)
> Z-729-22 Delivery weight 5.8 lbs. $31.99

Here is how you would fill out the second section of the order form.

PAGE NUMBER	NAME OF ITEM	CATALOG NUMBER		SIZE	COLOR (name & number)	HOW MANY	PRICE		WEIGHT
		letter	number				dollars	cents	
95	Pinstripe Bedspread	Z	729-21	Twin	pink 7	1	25	99	4.3 lbs.

On the order form, the heading PAGE NUMBER asks for the catalog page number on which you found the entry for the bedspread. The name of the item is the heading for the entry—"Pinstripe Bedspread." The catalog number for the twin bedspread is Z-729-21. The size of the spread you want is twin. The color you want is pink, and the color code number is 7. The bedspread costs $25.99 and weighs 4.3 pounds (lbs.). In the catalog entry, you can find all the information you need to fill out the order form.

Total Price and Total Weight

Sometimes you may want to order more than one item from a catalog. For example, besides buying a bedspread, you might also want to buy some sheets. Then your order form would look like this:

PAGE NUMBER	NAME OF ITEM	CATALOG NUMBER		SIZE	COLOR	HOW MANY	PRICE		WEIGHT
		letter	number		(name & number)		dollars	cents	
95	Pinstripe Bedspread	Z	729-21	Twin	pink 7	1	25	99	4.3 lbs.
106	Monogram Sheet Set	Z	716-03	Twin	blue 30	1	40	00	3.6 lbs.
							65	99	7.9 lbs.
							TOTAL PRICE FOR ITEMS		TOTAL WEIGHT

When you order two or more items through the mail, you must add all the prices in the price column to get the *total price for items.* Then write the total price in the space marked TOTAL PRICE FOR ITEMS at the bottom of the price column. In this example, the total price for items equals the price of the bedspread ($25.99) plus the price of the sheet ($40.00). The total price is $65.99. The total price for items, or total for goods, is the sum of the prices of all the items you want to buy. Another name for total price for items is *item total.*

When you order two or more items through the mail, you must add the delivery weights that you have entered in the weight column. The sum of the weights is the *total weight.* Write the total weight at the bottom of the weight column. In the example above, the total weight equals the weight of the bedspread (4.3 lbs.) plus the weight of the sheets (3.6 lbs.). The total weight is 7.9 lbs.

Filling Out Order Forms

If you want to buy an item through the mail, you must fill out the order form in the catalog. You know that an order form has three sections:

1. Shopper information
2. Item information
3. Total cost of the order

You have learned how to fill in shopper information and item information.

Exercise 1

Read the catalog entry below. It is taken from page 67 of the catalog.

A. Wingback Armchair. Hardwood frame. Strong string support. Loose pillow back padded with foam. Reversible seat cushion. Cotton-padded arms. 29 by 31 by 31 inches high.
Colors: 24 coffee; 82 sea green
R 792 Delivery weight 50 lbs. $260.00

Suppose you want to buy the armchair described in the entry. You want it in sea green. Fill out the order form on the next page. For the shopper information, give your own name, address and phone number. Use the catalog entry above to find the item information that you need to fill out section two of the order form.

ORDER FORM

Shopper Information

AREA CODE ( )	HOME PHONE NUMBER
NAME (first, middle initial, last)	
ADDRESS	
CITY/STATE	ZIP CODE

Item Information

PAGE NUMBER	NAME OF ITEM	CATALOG NUMBER		SIZE	COLOR (name & number)	HOW MANY	PRICE		WEIGHT
		letter	number				dollars	cents	

Exercise 2

Look at the completed order forms that follow. In each case, the shopper is buying two or more items. You know that to figure the total price for items the shopper has to add the prices of all the items ordered. To figure total weight, the shopper has to add the weights of all the items ordered. For each order form, add the prices in the PRICE column. Print your answer in the box marked TOTAL PRICE FOR ITEMS. Add the weights in the WEIGHT column. Print your answer in the box marked TOTAL WEIGHT. The first one has been done for you as an example.

1.

PAGE NUMBER	NAME OF ITEM	CATALOG NUMBER		SIZE	COLOR (name & number)	HOW MANY	PRICE		WEIGHT
		letter	number				dollars	cents	
465	Warm-up Jacket	Z	525	Large	royal blue 36	1	12	99	1.1 lbs.
498	Hooded Sweatshirt	Z	516	Medium	red 03	1	16	00	1.1 lbs.
							28	99	2.2 lbs.
							TOTAL PRICE FOR ITEMS		TOTAL WEIGHT

2.

PAGE NUMBER	NAME OF ITEM	CATALOG NUMBER		SIZE	COLOR	HOW MANY	PRICE		WEIGHT
		letter	number		(name & number)		dollars	cents	
440	Flannel shirt	S	543	Small	forest green 32	1	18	00	1.2 lbs.
441	Quilted parka	P	518	large	tan 22	1	100	00	2.3 lbs.
426	Workboots	Z	611	10	brown 14	1	65	00	3.4 lbs.

TOTAL PRICE FOR ITEMS | TOTAL WEIGHT

3.

PAGE NUMBER	NAME OF ITEM	CATALOG NUMBER		SIZE	COLOR	HOW MANY	PRICE		WEIGHT
		letter	number		(name & number)		dollars	cents	
419	Bowling ball	T	940	12	black	1	34	25	13.1 lbs.
419	Bowling shoes	T	943	7	powder blue	1	14	50	3.2 lbs.
421	Bowling bag	S	948		cocoa brown	1	24	00	2.3 lbs.

TOTAL PRICE FOR ITEMS | TOTAL WEIGHT

4.

PAGE NUMBER	NAME OF ITEM	CATALOG NUMBER letter	CATALOG NUMBER number	SIZE	COLOR (name & number)	HOW MANY	PRICE dollars	PRICE cents	WEIGHT
37	Patio table	R	654		white 09	1	95	00	13.0 lbs.
37	Set of 4 chairs	R	658		white 09	1	83	00	11.3 lbs.
41	Table umbrella	R	345		green/yellow 56	1	16	00	4.2 lbs.
42	Table cloth (patio)	R	360		yellow 45	1	7	00	1.6 lbs.

TOTAL PRICE FOR ITEMS		TOTAL WEIGHT

4

Closing In

Preview Words*/Chapter 4*

Study the words in the box. Then read the sentences below with your teacher. Look carefully at the words in boldface type.

clutching	flashlight	necklaces	straining
collar	hooves	robbery	throttle
cruising	Indian	rodeo	touched
dangerous	mountains	scrambling	trouble
finally	nearby	silver	yawning

1. Rita and Jeff were **cruising** across Wyoming.
2. The sign said "All American **Indian** Days."
3. The sign said that there would be a **rodeo** that day.
4. He turned the **throttle**, and the bike jumped forward.
5. Rita bent down to tie the rope to Mop's **collar**.
6. Jeff **finally** had to pick Mop up and carry her.
7. They were passing a store that sold Indian **necklaces**.
8. Rita saw a **silver** necklace in the window.
9. She **touched** her new necklace and smiled.
10. A moment later, he was **scrambling** to his feet.
11. "Oh, that looks so **dangerous**!" Rita said.
12. You have to watch out for those **hooves**.
13. I'm awfully sorry that she made so much **trouble**.
14. The road went up and up through the **mountains**.
15. They hid in the woods **nearby** to wait until dark.
16. She was upset about the **robbery** at the museum.
17. Ken and Steve were **straining** to hear.
18. "OK," Rita said, **yawning**. "I'm tired too."
19. Steve and Ken crawled closer, each **clutching** a big knife.
20. He shined his **flashlight** around the campsite.

Rita and Jeff were cruising across Wyoming. The land was open and rolling, and they could see for miles and miles. They could see in a big circle all around them, where the land met the sky.

They felt so free and happy, as if they were flying. They just cruised along under that big deep blue sky. They were in cow country now, passing great herds of cows. They saw sheep, too. This was the Wild West, just like on TV! All they needed were some cowboys.

Just at lunch time, they rolled into the city of Sheridan. They found the streets packed with cars. There were crowds of people everywhere, talking and smiling. When Jeff stopped to wait for traffic, he turned around to talk to Rita. "What's going on? It looks like a party!"

Rita shrugged her shoulders. Then she spotted a sign hung over the street and pointed to it. The sign said

ALL AMERICAN INDIAN DAYS
SHERIDAN, WYOMING
RODEO TODAY

Just then, the traffic moved on, and Jeff pulled into the line of cars. Rita hoped that he would stop somewhere in the city. The All American Indian Days sounded like fun! If they went to the rodeo they would get to see some cowboys after all.

Now Jeff was riding alongside the traffic, next to the parked cars. He loved to do that when there was a lot of traffic. He liked to slip through when all those big, fat cars had to wait.

He was looking for a parking space, but the cars were

parked very tightly, and every space was full. Then up ahead he saw a space just big enough for a bike. He turned the throttle, and the bike jumped forward, past two more cars in the line of waiting traffic. A van was sitting, waiting for the traffic to move, right next to the parking space he wanted. It was very tight, but he got by the van. Then he slid into the parking space.

In the van that Jeff had just passed were two men. Suddenly one of the men pointed at Jeff and Rita. "Look! Hey, Steve, look!" the man said quickly. "It's them, over there on the motorcycle!"

"No!" Steve said. "It couldn't be!"

"Yes, it is!" Ken said. "I knew them as soon as I saw them. See, there's the dog! The guy is taking the dog out of his jacket! It's them!"

Steve sat back in the driver's seat and rubbed his hand over his face. "OK, OK, Ken," he said, "I saw them. You're right, it's them."

"You said they were going to stay in Chicago!" Ken went on. "You said they would be there for a few days! Well, they should still be there. And then you said they were going to head right for California. Then what are they doing here? What are they doing here right on our tail?"

"Well, maybe they changed their plans," Steve said.

"Plans! What plans? I tell you, they're following us!"

On the sidewalk, Jeff and Rita were taking off their helmets. Rita got out the rope for Mop and bent down to tie it to the dog's collar. Then they walked away, down the sidewalk.

Just then the traffic began to move again. Steve began to pull the van forward with the traffic. "Wait, let me out!" Ken said. "I'm going to follow them! I want to find out where they're going!"

"All right," Steve said. "I'll try to find a place to park."

"Right," Ken said as he jumped out of the van. He walked down the street after Rita and Jeff, being careful not to let them see him.

All the people on the street seemed to be going the same way. Jeff and Rita walked along, following the other people to the rodeo. The closer they got, the more people there were on the street. Jeff held tightly to Mop's rope, but he finally had to pick her up and carry her.

Ken was still following them, but it was getting harder and harder for him to keep up with them. He kept losing sight of them in the crowds of people.

Rita was looking into the store windows as they walked along. Now they were passing a store that sold Indian things. Rita saw a silver necklace in the window. "Oh, Jeff, look at that necklace. Isn't it pretty? Let's go into the store and look at it," Rita said, pulling Jeff toward the door.

"OK," Jeff said as they walked into the store. "Anything to get out of this crowd."

They looked at all the necklaces, and Rita tried some on. "They're all so pretty," she said, "how can I pick out just one?"

At that moment Ken was walking by the store, trying to see Jeff and Rita in the crowd on the street. He didn't look into the window of the store as he hurried past.

"Look at this one, Jeff," Rita was saying as she held up one necklace. It had a tiny carving of a bird with its wings spread. "This one makes me think of being free, of flying, like being on the bike. And the silver work is so pretty." She put the necklace around her neck. "Isn't it nice?" she asked Jeff, turning around so that he could see it.

Jeff looked at the necklace carefully and ran his finger over the carving. "Almost as pretty as you are," he said, giving Rita a quick hug.

Out on the street, Ken had walked on past them. He was hurrying through the crowd, looking for them. Where were they? How could they have got so far ahead of him? How could they have got away?

They must have seen him, he thought. They must be hiding. Maybe they were hiding in a store. He turned around and walked back the way he had come, looking carefully into every store window.

At that moment, Jeff and Rita were just coming out onto the sidewalk again. Jeff put Mop down and held her by the rope. They started to walk down the sidewalk toward the rodeo, but Mop pulled them toward the street.

They stepped off the sidwalk, between two parked cars. When Rita looked back toward the store where they had been, she saw Ken looking in the store window. "Look," she called to Jeff, "see that man over there? Where have I seen him before?"

"Who knows?" Jeff said. "It could have been anywhere. We've seen a lot of people since we left New York." He picked Mop up and put her in the front of his shirt. They crossed the street, and Ken went on down the sidewalk, looking in the store windows.

Jeff and Rita followed the crowds of people until they came to a big grandstand. They got tickets and went in.

The rodeo had already started. They found seats near the front, where they could look down into the ring. Two men were running around in the ring, dressed up as clowns. Rita and Jeff looked at each other. Clowns at a rodeo?

On the other side of the ring, behind a big door, some men were getting ready. Jeff and Rita couldn't see what the men were doing, but they could hear something moving around.

Suddenly, bang! The door opened and a huge bull ran out into the ring. Rita gasped and grabbed Jeff's arm. There was a man on its back!

The bull ran forward, then turned sharply. The man hung on with one hand, while he waved his hat in the air with the other. The bull turned again and twisted its body high in the air. The man fell off the bull's back, hit the ground, and lay still.

The clowns ran toward him. One of the clowns danced around in front of the bull, trying to make it chase him. He ran across the ring with the bull right behind him. The other clown helped the man get up. The man walked slowly back toward the doors, while the crowd cheered.

Rita and Jeff cheered too. They watched as the bull was taken out of the ring. Then they saw another man getting ready. Bang! The big door opened and the bull jumped out into the ring. Jump! Twist! Jump! And the man was off his back and lying in the dirt. The man jumped up and headed for the side of the ring.

Rita and Jeff cheered with the crowd. Jeff talked to an old man sitting next to him. The old man had been in rodeos in the old days, and he told Jeff what it was like to ride a bull. Rita just sat back in her seat and looked around. It was fun just to be here. Here she was in Sheridan, Wyoming. It sure was a long way from New York City! What a time they were having. What a great trip! She touched her new necklace and smiled. She would remember this trip as long as she lived.

At that moment Ken was getting back in the van with Steve. "Well, did you follow them?" Steve asked. "What were they up to?"

"I followed them for a little way," Ken said, "but then they must have spotted me. They hid on me. One moment they were there, and the next moment they were gone."

"Oh come on," Steve said as he pulled the van out into the traffic again. "They just came to watch the rodeo. They'll be here all afternoon. By the time the rodeo is over we'll be most of the way to Yellowstone Park. We won't see them again." The van headed out of the city of Sheridan.

In the grandstand, Jeff and Rita were watching the rodeo. Another man got ready behind the big door. Bang! The door opened and the bull roared out, twisting and jumping. The man held onto its back and waved his hat. Suddenly the man was gone. A moment later he was scrambling to his feet, fighting to get away from the bull's pounding hooves. The clowns were dancing around the bull, waving their arms.

"Oh that looks so dangerous!" Rita said. She leaned across Jeff to ask the old man, "Did you ever get hurt?"

The old man laughed. "Oh sure, I've been hurt quite a few times. You have to watch out for those hooves. If you get kicked . . ." He rubbed his head, remembering. "I got kicked in the head once, and I didn't wake up for two days. Yes, you have to watch out for those hooves. The clowns have to be quick too."

Now another man was getting ready. They could see his head and shoulders over the door. He was looking down as he got onto the bull's back. He grabbed his hat, then nodded his head. Bang! The door opened and the bull roared out into the ring.

Suddenly Mop woke up. Quick as a flash, she jumped out of Jeff's shirt and ran down to the front of the grandstand. She put her front feet on the railing and started to bark at the bull in the ring. "Darned dog!" Jeff shouted as he jumped up to run after her. He grabbed for her and missed. His hand bumped her, and she fell into the ring.

"Mop!" Rita screamed. Mop lay on the ground, not moving. The bull roared toward her, jumping and twisting. The man flew off his back and landed on the ground. The bull turned and ran away from the man and the clowns. Then it turned again, running right for Mop. The pounding hooves were coming closer and closer.

Mop jumped up and started to run—right toward the bull! The bull pounded by her, its big hooves kicking up the dust as it passed. For a moment Mop was gone in the

cloud of dust. Then they saw her again, running after the bull and barking short little barks. The bull turned again and ran toward the little dog with its head down. "Mop! Mop, come back!" Rita screamed.

The clowns ran toward the bull, trying to cut it off. More men ran out into the ring, heading for the bull, waving their hats and shouting, "Let's go! Back to the doors! Hey! Hey!" They got the bull to go back through the door. Mop ran right after them, barking the whole time. One of the clowns bent down and picked her up and carried her back across the ring. The crowd was laughing and cheering.

Jeff turned and called to Rita, "*You* come down here and take her! I don't even want to *know* that dog!" As the clown held Mop up to Rita, Jeff turned his back.

"You'd better get this dog out of here, Miss," the clown said. He had a big smile painted on his face, but Rita could see that he was very angry.

"Yes sir," Rita said. "I'm awfully sorry that she made so much trouble."

"Well we were lucky this time," the clown said. "No one got hurt. But they don't allow dogs in the grandstand. It gets the bulls upset."

"We'll take her out," Rita said. "Thank you for saving her." The clown waved and walked off across the ring.

When Rita turned to Jeff, his face was tight with anger. "So we've been thrown out of another place, have we?" he snapped. "All because of that darned dog!"

"I'll take her out," Rita said. "You stay and watch the rodeo."

"No, that's all right. Come on. If we get going we can make Yellowstone Park tonight."

They left the city and hit the highway. The road went

up and up through the mountains. It was fun to race along on the motorcycle, up and up and up, through cuts in the mountain and by steep cliffs. Then over the top and down, down the other side. After all the flat land they had been through, this was great.

Now they were getting near Yellowstone Park. They started to look for a campground.

The van was getting near Yellowstone, too.

"I'm getting tired," Steve said. He pointed to a sign by the side of the road ahead. "Let's stop at that campground up there."

"It's not even dark yet!" Ken said. "We've got to make some miles! I want to get ahead of those two on the motorcycle."

"Oh come on," Steve said, "they'll be at that rodeo all day and half the night. Look, the van is loaded too heavy for these mountains. It's beginning to overheat." He pulled off the road into the campground. "I'm stopping. It'll be OK. We won't see that motorcycle again."

Just as the two men pulled into a campsite, before they had even got out of the van, they saw the motorcycle go by. "Look," Ken said, grabbing Steve's arm, "it's them!"

"You're right, it *is* them! What are they doing here?" Steve asked. "How did they catch up with us already?"

"I told you, they never went to that rodeo. They're following us!"

"I still can't believe it," Steve said. "They just don't look like cops."

"Well let's check them out," Ken said. "Then maybe you'll believe it."

The two men got out of the van and walked carefully through the campground, looking for Jeff and Rita.

When they spotted their campsite, they hid in the woods nearby to wait until it got dark.

Jeff and Rita were setting up their tent. Then Jeff made supper for a change, while Rita started a fire. They sat by the fire, eating and watching the night come. Even Mop was sitting still. It was very peaceful.

Ken and Steve crawled through the woods toward them. Now the men were close enough to hear Rita and Jeff talking. They couldn't hear everything, but they could hear a word here and there.

"I was just thinking," Rita said, "maybe I should call home."

"Why?" Jeff asked.

"Oh, I just want to know how Mom is. She was so upset about the robbery at the museum where she works."

Ken and Steve were straining to hear. "What did she say?" Ken asked quietly. "Could you hear her?"

"She said something about calling someone," Steve told him, "then something about a robbery."

"A robbery!" Ken said. "See, I told you!"

"Shut up, I want to hear this!" Steve crawled closer to Rita and Jeff.

"Can you believe it?" Rita was saying. "Mom told me that they got twenty paintings. They put paper around each painting and tied them up with string. Then they walked right out of the museum with them." She shook her head. "They must have had a van. But no one saw them."

Steve had heard enough. He backed up quickly and waved for Ken to follow him. They crawled back into the woods, where Rita and Jeff couldn't hear them. "You were right!" Steve told Ken. "They know all about us! They know how many paintings we got and how we put paper around them and everything. She even said something about the van. They must have been following us ever since we left New York City. They must have thought we wouldn't spot them."

"Well what are we going to do?" Ken asked.

"I don't know," Steve said. "Maybe if we left right now . . . Maybe if we holed up somewhere . . ."

"That won't work! If they've followed us this far, they can follow us anywhere!" Ken said. "We'll have to get rid of them!"

"But—"

"They're cops! It's them or us!" Ken said. And Steve nodded.

Back at the campfire, Jeff was picking up the supper dishes. "You can call your mother tomorrow," he was saying. "I'm too tired to go looking for a phone tonight. OK?"

"OK," Rita said, yawning. "I'm tired too. We'll all sleep well tonight. Come on, Mop."

Soon it was quiet in their tent. Steve and Ken crawled closer through the woods, each clutching a big knife.

They waited while the people in the other campsites went to bed. One by one, the campsites went dark. At last there was no sound but the breezes in the trees. It was time to move in.

Slowly, carefully, Ken and Steve got up. They walked quietly to the edge of the woods and looked carefully around the campsite. Everything was quiet. They stepped out of the woods and walked quietly across the campsite toward the tent. Ken waved Steve around to the other side of the tent. Then carefully he bent down and peeked in through the tent window. He stood up and nodded to Steve.

They stood there for a moment, one on each side of

the tent. They could hear Rita and Jeff breathing. Steve was waiting for Ken to make a move. At last Ken lifted his knife, and Steve lifted his knife, too. They raised them high, getting ready to stab down into the little tent.

"Woof! Woof!" Mop started to bark. The noise was so sudden that both men jumped back, away from the tent. "Woof! Woof! Woof!"

"What's the matter, Mop?" Rita asked sleepily. "What is it, girl? Jeff, I think Mop smells something. There's something outside!"

Ken and Steve looked at each other. They quickly ran across the campsite and dove into the woods. Behind them they heard Jeff unzip the tent. "OK, OK, Mop," Jeff was saying. "Quiet down! You'll wake everyone up. Take it easy, I'm going to check it out."

"Be careful, Jeff," Rita said.

"Oh don't worry," Jeff said as he crawled out of the tent. He shined his flashlight around the campsite. "See, there's nothing out here!"

Mop was still barking. She jumped out of the tent and ran toward the woods, but Jeff grabbed her as she ran by. "Oh, no, you don't," he said. "I'm not going to run after you in those woods in the dark." He threw Mop back into the tent. He shined the flashlight around the campsite one more time, then crawled back into the tent himself. "I don't know," he told Rita. "There wasn't a thing out there. If she barks again and wakes everyone up, we could get thrown out of here."

"Now, Jeff," Rita started to say.

"No, I mean it! That dog has been nothing but trouble on this trip. I've had it with her! Bringing her along was stupid. We'll have to think of something to do with her tomorrow."

At that moment, Ken and Steve were making their way back to their own campsite. "I didn't know what we were up against!" Steve said. "They really know what they're doing! Bringing that dog along was smart!"

"Well we'll think of something," Ken said. "We'll get them tomorrow."

Comprehension Questions/Chapter 4

Directions. Answer these questions about the chapter you have just read. Put an *x* in the box beside the best answer to each question.

1. (B) Why did Jeff and Rita go into the store in Sheridan?

☐ a. To hide from Ken
☐ b. To tie Mop up
☐ c. To buy some food for lunch
☐ d. To look at a silver necklace

2. (C) What happened next after Rita and Jeff went into the store?

☐ a. Ken got out of the van.
☐ b. Ken walked by the store.
☐ c. Jeff and Rita crossed the street.
☐ d. Ken looked into the store window.

3. (D) Why were there clowns at the rodeo?

☐ a. Just to make the crowd laugh
☐ b. To help the cowboys get onto the bulls
☐ c. To help the cowboys get out of the way of the bulls after they fell
☐ d. To show people to their seats

4. (A) The clowns ran toward the bull, trying to *cut it off* before it got to Mop. What does this mean?

- ☐ a. Kill it
- ☐ b. Cut off its head
- ☐ c. Stop it
- ☐ d. Get rid of it

5. (C) Which of these things happened last?

- ☐ a. The bull ran toward Mop.
- ☐ b. The clown picked Mop up.
- ☐ c. Mop barked at the bull.
- ☐ d. Jeff yelled at Rita.

6. (E) When they got to Yellowstone Park, how did Rita and Jeff end up at the same campground as the two men?

- ☐ a. It just happened to work out that way.
- ☐ b. They saw which campground Ken and Steve had gone into.
- ☐ c. They were following the two men.
- ☐ d. The two men were following them.

7. (A) Steve said, "Maybe we should leave right now. Maybe we should *hole up* somewhere." What did he mean?

- ☐ a. Get into a hole in the ground
- ☐ b. Dig a deep hole in the ground
- ☐ c. Find a hiding place
- ☐ d. Climb into the van

8. (D) What made Steve believe that Jeff and Rita were really police?

- ☐ a. Ken talked him into it.
- ☐ b. He thought he heard Rita telling all about the robbery he and Ken had pulled.
- ☐ c. He thought he heard Rita telling the man at the rodeo that they were police.
- ☐ d. He saw Jeff's gun.

9. (B) How did Ken and Steve plan to kill Rita and Jeff?

- ☐ a. By running over their tent with the van
- ☐ b. By stabbing them in their tent with knives
- ☐ c. By throwing them in front of the bull
- ☐ d. By shooting them

10. (E) What important thing did Mop do in this part of the story?

- ☐ a. She saved Jeff's and Rita's lives by scaring away Ken and Steve.
- ☐ b. She scared the bull at the rodeo.
- ☐ c. She woke up everyone at the campground.
- ☐ d. She made Jeff mad by barking at the bull.

Skills Used to Answer Questions

A. Recognizing Words in Context B. Recalling Facts
C. Keeping Events in Order D. Making Inferences
E. Understanding Main Ideas

Commas in Direct Address

You know that a comma tells you where to pause in a sentence. You have learned how to use commas in compound sentences, in lists of items, and in sentences with quotations. Now you will learn how to use commas in *direct address.* Read the two sentences below.

Sir, are you ready?

We are happy to see you, Mrs. Santos.

These two sentences name the person being directly spoken to. Both *sir* and *Mrs. Santos* are said to be in *direct address.* Words in direct address may be either names or words by which people are called. For example, a person could be called *friend, mister* or *son* when being spoken to. In the first example above, the words *are you ready?* are spoken—or addressed—to Sir. In the second example, the words *We are happy to see you* are addressed to Mrs. Santos.

Now read the two sentences below. Each contains a name in direct address. Notice where the comma is placed in each sentence.

Please close the door, Carmen.
Carmen, please close the door.

You can see that the comma used with a name in direct address sets the name off from the rest of the sentence. In the first example, the person's name, Carmen, is at the end of the sentence. The comma is placed after the word that comes right before the name. The comma tells you to pause slightly before going on to the name of the person being addressed. In the second example, the name Carmen is at the beginning of the sentence. The comma is placed after the name. It tells you to pause before going on to the rest of the sentence.

Exercise 1

The sentences below contain words and names in direct address, but they have no commas. Copy each sentence on the line provided, putting in the comma where it is needed. Remember that the comma used in direct address sets off the name of the person from the rest of the sentence. The first sentence has been done for you as an example.

1. It is time for bed Jackie.

   It is time for bed, Jackie.

2. Kathy turn off the stove.

   ____

3. Where is your purse Jean?

   ____

4. Dad can I go to the party?

   ____

5. Watch your step Kevin.

   ____

6. Did you make the cake Suzanne?

   ____

7. Rick wait for me!

   ____

Making Your Own Direct Address Sentences

If you are given the words that are spoken and the name of the person being spoken to, you can write your own direct address sentences. Just copy the words that are spoken and place the name of the person being addressed at the beginning or the end. Use a comma to set the name of the person off from the rest of the sentence. Look at the example below.

words: Can you fix the lawn mower?
person: Maria

New sentences:

Maria, can you fix the lawn mower?
Can you fix the lawn mower, Maria?

Exercise 2

Now it is your turn to write some sentences using names in direct address. For each set of spoken words and names given below, make up two sentences with the names used in direct address. Write the sentences on the lines provided. On the top line, place the name of the person being spoken to at the beginning of the sentence. On the bottom line, place the name of the person at the end of the sentence. The first one has been done for you as an example.

1. Eat your pie. Matt

Matt, eat your pie.

Eat your pie, Matt.

2. It's your turn now. David

3. Have you met Susan? Katie

4. Stay in the house. Mona

5. Make your bed. son

6. Did you feed the baby? Ron

7. It is time to go. Will

Total Cost: Part One

You know that when you buy an item through the mail you must fill out the order form in the mail order catalog. You have learned how to enter shopper information and item information on the form. Now you will learn how to figure the *total cost of your order.*

The total cost of an order is the amount of money that must be paid to the company. The total cost is the sum of three prices:

1. Total price for items
2. Sales tax
3. Shipping charges

You already know how to find the total price for items. In this chapter you will learn how to figure sales tax.

Orders from National Companies

Suppose you place a mail order with a big national company. A national company has stores and outlets all over the country. You must pay sales tax on orders from national companies. An order form in a national company's catalog has a box marked "sales tax." The catalog also has a sales tax table.

Look at the completed order form on the next page. The shopper is buying a sleeping bag, a tent and a flashlight from a national company.

In the example, the shopper's total price for items is $110.00. It is the sum of the price of the tent ($60.00), the price of the sleeping bag ($40.00), and the price of the flashlight ($10.00). The amount 110.00 is entered in the box marked TOTAL PRICE FOR ITEMS.

ORDER FORM

Shopper Information

AREA CODE	HOME PHONE NUMBER
(205)	863-6121

NAME (first, middle initial, last): Maria L. Brown

ADDRESS: 45 Maple Street

CITY/STATE: Birmingham, Alabama — ZIP CODE: 35201

☑ Check Method of Payment

☐ I have enclosed a check or money order.

☐ Charge to my: (Circle one) master charge VISA

Card #:

Expiration date:

Signature (as shown on credit card)

Item Information

PAGE NUMBER	NAME OF ITEM	CATALOG NUMBER letter	CATALOG NUMBER number	SIZE	COLOR (name & number)	HOW MANY	PRICE dollars	PRICE cents	WEIGHT
65	Sleeping bag	Z	496-31		green 43	1	40	00	
114	Tent	Z	643-11		blue 5	1	60	00	
123	Flashlight	Z	489-42		red 24	1	10	00	
						TOTAL PRICE FOR ITEMS	110	00	TOTAL WEIGHT:

Order Totals

TOTAL PRICE FOR ITEMS	110	00
SALES TAX	4	40
SHIPPING AND HANDLING		
TOTAL COST	114	40

Once you know the total price for items, you can use the sales tax table in the catalog to figure your tax. Part of a sales tax table is shown below.

STATE	SALES TAX RATE	STATE	SALES TAX RATE
Alabama	4%	Colorado	3½%
Alaska	0	Connecticut	7½%
Arizona	4%	Delaware	0
Arkansas	3%	District of Columbia	6%
California	5%	Florida	5%

There are two columns of information in each section of the sales tax table. The first is an alphabetical listing of states. To find your sales tax, you must first look for the state in which you live. The second column lists the *sales tax rate* for each state. The sales tax rate is a percentage that tells you how much tax you must pay on each dollar of the total price for items.

For example, suppose you live in Florida. You can see that according to the table the sales tax rate for Florida is 5%. That means that you must pay 5¢ on every dollar of the total price for items. If the total for items is $1.00, you must pay 5¢ sales tax. If it is $2.00, you must pay 10¢, and so on. If the total for goods is $20.00, you must pay 100¢, or $1.00, in sales tax.

Look back at the order for a sleeping bag, a tent and a flashlight on page 137.

Look at the personal information on the order form. In what state does the shopper, Maria Brown, live? Print your answer here:

____

What is the sales tax rate for Maria Brown's state? Find the correct sales tax rate from the table. Print it here:

____

Look at the box marked TOTAL PRICE FOR ITEMS on Maria Brown's order form. Copy her total price for items here:

____

The total price for items of Maria Brown's order is $110.00. Look for Alabama on the sales tax table. You can see that the Alabama sales tax rate is 4%. That means Maria Brown must pay 4¢ on every dollar of the total price for items, which is $110.00. Maria Brown's sales tax is 440¢, or $4.40. The amount 4.40 is entered in the box marked SALES TAX on the order form.

Orders from Local Companies

Suppose you place a mail order with a small local company. A local company has stores and outlets in only one state or region of the country. You do not pay sales tax on an order from a local company unless you live in the state or region in which the company is located.

Look at the completed order form below. The shopper is buying a backpack and an army knife from a local company. The company is in Maine.

Item Information

PAGE NUMBER	NAME OF ITEM	CATALOG NUMBER letter	CATALOG NUMBER number	SIZE	COLOR (name & number)	HOW MANY	PRICE dollars	PRICE cents	WEIGHT
46	Day pack	Q	6239		red	1	16	00	
51	Swiss army knife	Q	5148		navy blue	1	20	00	
							36	00	
							TOTAL PRICE FOR ITEMS		TOTAL WEIGHT

Order Totals

TOTAL PRICE FOR ITEMS	36	00
5% SALES TAX ON SHIPMENTS TO MAINE		
SHIPPING AND HANDLING		
TOTAL COST		

The sales tax line on the form says "5% sales tax on shipments to Maine." That means that a shopper who lives in Maine must pay sales tax. The Maine shopper must pay 5¢ on every dollar of the total price for items. The item total of this order is $36.00. The Maine shopper must pay 5¢ x 36.00, or $1.80 sales tax.

A shopper who does not live in Maine pays no sales tax. The shopper in the example lives in Provo, Utah. He pays no sales tax on his order. He leaves the sales tax line blank.

Suppose the shopper lived in Seattle, Washington. Would he pay sales tax on his order? Circle your answer.

Yes No

Figuring Sales Tax

You must pay sales tax on all mail orders from national companies. On mail orders from local companies, you pay sales tax only if the company is in your state or region.

You have now learned how to figure the amount of sales tax you must pay on an order. Local companies give sales tax information and rates right on their order forms. National companies print sales tax tables in their catalogs. A buyer uses a sales tax table to find out the sales tax rate for his or her state.

The sales tax line on an order form tells you if you must pay sales tax on your order. Sometimes the line just says "sales tax." Then you must pay tax no matter where you live. Sometimes the line lists one or more states. It gives the tax rate for each state listed. Then you must pay sales tax only if you live in one of the states listed. You must pay the rate given for your state.

Exercise 1

Next to each number in this exercise is a sales tax line taken from the order form of a *local company*. Below each sales tax line is information about shoppers. Each of those lines tells where a shopper lives. Read each sales tax line. Then read the shopper information below it. Decide whether or not the shopper must pay sales tax. If he or she must, print the sales tax rate on the line provided. If the shopper owes no sales tax, print "No Tax" on the line. Remember that the sales tax rate tells you how much tax the shopper must pay on every dollar of an order. The first one has been done for you as an example.

1. DELIVERY TO VERMONT ADDRESS, ADD 4% SALES TAX.

   a. The shopper lives in Vermont. 4% tax

   b. The shopper lives in California. no tax

2. ADD 5% TAX IF DELIVERED IN MASSACHUSETTS.

   a. The shopper lives in Michigan. ______

   b. The shopper lives in Massachusetts. ______

3. FOR DELIVERY IN WISCONSIN, ADD 5% SALES TAX; IN ILLINOIS 5%; IN IOWA 4%.

   a. The shopper lives in Illinois. ______

   b. The shopper lives in Wisconsin. ______

   c. The shopper lives in Missouri. ______

   d. The shopper lives in Iowa. ______

Exercise 2

Part of a sales tax table is shown below.

STATE	SALES TAX RATE	STATE	SALES TAX RATE
Maine	5%	New Hampshire	0
Maryland	5%	New Jersey	6%
Massachusetts	5%	New Mexico	3½%
Michigan	4%	New York	4%
Minnesota	6%	North Carolina	4%
Mississippi	5%	North Dakota	4%
Montana	0	Ohio	5½%

Use the table to find the sales tax rate for each of the following orders. The orders are from a *national company.* Follow these steps:

1. Find the state you need in the column marked STATE.
2. Find the sales tax rate for that state in the column to the right, marked SALES TAX RATE.

Remember that the sales tax rate tells you how much tax you must pay on each dollar of your order. Print the sales tax rate on the line provided. The first one has been done for you as an example.

1. You live in New Mexico. The sales tax rate for your order is 3 ½ % .

2. You live in Mississippi. The sales tax rate for your order is __________ .

3. You live in Massachusetts. The sales tax rate for your order is ______________________________ .

4. You live in New Hampshire. The sales tax rate for your order is ______________________________ .

5. You live in Ohio. The sales tax rate for your order is ______________________________ .

5

The Cobra Strikes

Preview Words/*Chapter 5*

Study the words in the box. Then read the sentences below with your teacher. Look carefully at the words in boldface type.

bubbles	forcing	ranger	squeezed
builds	guard	report	sweat
cameras	knees	rescue	wheel
couple	mirror	screeching	wildly
famous	policemen	skidded	wrecked

1. They looked at the **famous** sights of Yellowstone.
2. Big **bubbles** came up to the top of the mud.
3. The steam **builds** up under the ground.
4. People were getting their **cameras** ready.
5. Mop danced around their feet, barking **wildly**.
6. They won't care about the stolen paintings . . . if we kill a **couple** of cops.
7. There weren't any **guard** rails at the edge of the highway.
8. As he slowed down, he looked in his **mirror**.
9. Now the car cut in front of him, **forcing** him over.
10. Their **knees** were almost on the road as the bike swung to the left.
11. Jeff broke out in a **sweat**.
12. The Cobra **skidded** across the highway.
13. The tires were **screeching** on the pavement.
14. He **squeezed** the clutch and let up on the throttle.
15. Ken held the **wheel** over hard.
16. Rita was looking back at the **wrecked** car.
17. We'll go back and tell the park **rangers**.
18. Two rangers and a **rescue** truck were on their way.
19. Two **policemen** were checking out the wrecked Cobra.
20. Well, we'll have to make a full **report**.

Ken and Steve were moving quietly in the dark. They packed up their camping things and loaded up the van. Then they drove out of the campground, very slowly, with their lights out. They drove a little way down the highway, until Ken said, "Here's a good place." They pulled the van in behind some bushes and turned off the motor.

They waited.

No one came down the road.

After they had waited a little longer, Ken said, "OK, they aren't following us. Let's go on with our plan." They drove on until they came to an old ranch, out in the middle of nowhere, with an old empty barn. "That's it," Ken said. "That looks just right."

They turned around and drove back to Yellowstone Park, to a campground on the other side of the park from Jeff and Rita. "Will you remember how to get back to that barn?" Steve asked as they pulled into the campground.

"I'll remember," Ken said. "Look, there's a good car right over there."

A brand new Cobra was parked next to a tent in the next campsite. "Leave this to me," Steve said as he quietly got out of the van. The van moved on down the road.

Steve moved quietly through the dark and got into the Cobra. Slowly, quietly, it rolled out of the campsite. A moment later the motor started and the car pulled quietly away. The people in the tent never woke up.

Steve followed the van back to the old ranch. Ken hid the van in the barn, then jumped into the car. "OK, we're ready for them," he said.

The next morning, Jeff and Rita were eating their breakfast. Mop was tied to the motorcycle, but she was pulling against her rope. She wanted to run around and sniff at things. She began to bark. "Shut up!" Jeff yelled.

"Oh, Jeff," Rita said, "you don't have to—"

"Don't you start in on me!" Jeff told her. "Last night was the last straw! Why was she barking like that in the middle of the night? I'll bet she woke up everyone in the campground! What got into her, anyway?"

"She smelled something outside," Rita said.

"There wasn't anything out here!" Jeff said. "No, I've had it with her! She has been nothing but trouble on this trip. Why do I have to take my honeymoon with a dog, anyway? We're going to send her the rest of the way on a train."

"No, Jeff!" Rita said. "She's *my* dog! I won't have her sent on a train like a package. I won't have her put in a box. She wouldn't like it. She thinks she's a person, not a dog."

"But we can't go anywhere with her along!" Jeff said. "We can't go to a restaurant. We can't go to a rodeo. We couldn't even stay at your aunt's house!"

"I don't think you *wanted* to stay at my aunt's house," Rita snapped. "I don't think you liked my aunt at all!"

"I liked her better than *you* did!" Jeff yelled. "You won't let anyone say a thing against that dog! But I'm saying it! She's going on the train to California! Better yet, let's put her on the train back to New York!"

"If she goes on a train, then I'm going too!" Rita yelled. "And New York would be fine!"

Steve and Ken were waiting, hidden behind some trees outside Yellowstone Park. "What's taking them so long?" Steve asked.

"They'll be here," Ken said. "We can't go after them.

The police must be looking for this car by now. We'll just wait."

"Are you sure we should go through with this?" Steve asked. "They don't seem to be following us this morning. Maybe they aren't cops. Maybe—"

"They're cops," Ken said.

At last Rita and Jeff got packed up. They drove out of the campground and on into Yellowstone Park—with Mop.

The park was already crowded with people. Rita and Jeff felt more at home with all the other people around. Bit by bit they forgot about their fight and started to look at the famous sights of Yellowstone.

They stopped to look at some hot springs. They stood by the side of the road, looking down into the mud. Bubble . . . bubble . . . bubble . . . Big bubbles came up to the top of the mud and broke, making the air smell like rotten eggs. Rita held her nose and laughed.

Outside the park, the Cobra was waiting. The two men in the car were not laughing.

Jeff and Rita got back on the motorcycle and rode slowly along with their helmets off. They liked the sights and sounds—and even the smells—of Yellowstone Park. "Wait until you see Old Faithful!" Jeff said.

They saw a sign that said

OLD FAITHFUL

PARK HERE

NEXT ERUPTION 10:27

Jeff parked the motorcycle in the parking lot. He looked at his watch and told Rita, "It's ten minutes past ten. We have to wait for seventeen minutes—more or less."

"Can they really tell just when it's going to go off?" Rita asked.

"Like I said—more or less. But Old Faithful always

goes off, just about once an hour. That's why they call it Old Faithful."

"Wow!" Rita looked around, but she could see nothing but flat ground. "It doesn't look like much."

"Just wait," Jeff said. "There are hot springs under the ground. There are lots of them around here. The steam from the hot springs builds up under the ground. It builds up and builds up, then, POW! It blows right up out of the ground."

The minutes went by. More and more cars pulled into the parking lot, and more and more people crowded around. It was 10:25. People were getting their cameras ready. It was 10:26. People waited, watching the hole in the ground. It was 10:27. Nothing happened.

Jeff checked his watch. "Like I said—they know when it will go off, more or less. Come on, Old Faithful."

Just then the ground began to rumble. Rumble . . . Rumble . . . The ground was shaking. Rumble . . . Suddenly sh-sh-SH-SH—a great blast of water and steam shot up out of the ground. Up—up—up, 150 feet in the air!

Rita just stood there staring at it, so Jeff grabbed the camera out of her hands and took a picture. Mop danced around their feet, barking wildly.

Then, just as suddenly, the water dropped. Lower . . . lower . . . It was gone. There was nothing there but a hole in the ground.

"Wow," Rita said, shaking her head. "I can't believe it. And I saw it with my own eyes." She turned to Jeff. "This trip has been so much fun," she said, giving him a hug. "I wish it would never end. But it will be fun in California—with you." Mop barked sharply, and Rita picked her up and patted her. "Don't worry, Mop, you're coming to California too," she said, smiling at Jeff.

Jeff just shrugged his shoulders, but at last he smiled too. "If we're all going to California we'd better get going," he said.

They pulled out of the parking lot. In a minute they were on the road, heading out of Yellowstone Park. They drove until they were out of the park and back on the highway, then roared on down the highway toward Idaho. They never even saw the Cobra parked by the side of the road.

"That's them!" Steve said.

"I see them," Ken said as he pulled out onto the road. "We'll just give them a minute to get away from

Yellowstone. Then we'll make our move."

Jeff and Rita were flying down the highway ahead of them. They were going through the mountains, up and up, climbing higher and higher. The wind rushed past them. Rita leaned back against the sissy bar and held on tight.

Now they were at the top. A few minutes later they passed a sign that said

WELCOME TO IDAHO

The Cobra passed the sign a minute later. "We're crossing a state line in a stolen car," Steve said. "We're getting into this deeper and deeper."

"Oh shut up!" Ken said. "Who cares about a stolen car when we have a van full of stolen paintings in that barn? And they won't care about the stolen paintings if we kill a couple of cops."

Now the motorcycle was running through a pass in the mountains. The tall mountains stood up all around them. Rita looked around, then made herself look straight ahead. The place scared her a little. The mountains were so tall, and the sides were so steep, and there weren't any guard rails at the edge of the highway. If they went off the road, it would be down, down, down. She looked back at the car coming up behind them. "That car is moving right along," she thought. "*That* driver doesn't care about guard rails!"

"Now's the time!" Ken was saying as he came up behind them. "Down there, by that bend in the road! There's a good steep cliff there!"

"Maybe we shouldn't—" Steve started to say. But then he looked at Ken's face. It was a mask of hate. Steve didn't say anything more.

Jeff let the motorcycle fly down the side of the mountain. Now he was coming to a bend in the road. As he slowed down, he looked in his mirror. A car was in back of him, and it was coming closer—fast. "What's he up to?" Jeff asked himself. "I don't want to take that bend too fast—"

Roar! The Cobra pulled out to pass him. Now it was cutting in front of him, forcing him over—over to the side of the road. Jeff looked to the right. There was nothing there! Just a cliff and empty air.

Jeff turned the clutch—tap, tap—down to third gear. "Lean with me, Baby," he shouted as the bike slowed down suddenly. They leaned to the left—over, over—their knees almost on the road as the bike swung to the left. The bike came up as they cut behind the Cobra. Then over to the right, leaning hard, and they were around the Cobra and going on down the road.

Jeff could feel the sweat break out on him under his jacket. He could feel Mop shaking. She must have known that something was wrong. Jeff had just enough time to wonder about it. What *had* gone wrong? Why had that car cut him off like that?

Then the Cobra was on them again.

This time the Cobra did not try to pass the bike. It came up behind them, faster and faster. Jeff could see it in his mirror, getting bigger and bigger. In a moment it would hit them and push them right over the cliff.

Jeff leaned to the left to let the Cobra go by, but the car cut left too. Jeff cut right. The Cobra skidded, its tires screeching on the pavement. But it was right behind them.

The Cobra was coming closer and closer. Jeff had run out of time. In one last try, he pulled over as far to the right as he could. He squeezed the clutch and let up on the throttle. Tap, tap, tap—his left foot hit the shifter. Then he leaned left—over, over. Would the tires hold the road? Don't skid on me, he thought. Don't skid.

The bike went around in a U-turn. As they came around Jeff turned the throttle, and the engine roared. The bike came up and roared up the road, back the way they had come.

The Cobra tried to make the turn. It came around hard, tires screeching. Ken held the wheel over hard, fighting to keep the car on the road. The rear end swung around. "Watch out!" Steve yelled. But it was too late. The car skidded and rolled and hit a big rock on the side of the road. Crash! It came to a sudden stop on its side.

Jeff saw the crash in his mirror. He went on up the mountain a little way, then pulled over to the side of the road and stopped. He turned around in the seat and put one arm around Rita. "Don't look back," he said. "Are you OK?"

"Yes, I'm OK," Rita said in a shaky voice. "Is it over? What happened?"

"Yes, it's over. The car crashed down there. No one is

moving." Mop stuck her head up out of Jeff's jacket, and Jeff patted her. "It's all right now, Mop. Go back to sleep. It's all over."

Rita was looking back at the wrecked car. "Oh, Jeff, we should . . . we should go back and see if we can do anything for them."

"Go back? Are you crazy? We aren't going *near* that car! They were trying to kill us!"

"But why?"

"I don't know. Maybe they don't like bikes."

"But, Jeff, what are we going to *do?* We can't just leave them there."

"We'll go back to Yellowstone Park and tell the park rangers. They can take care of it." Jeff pushed Mop back down inside his jacket and started the motorcycle. There was nothing Rita could do but hang on.

As soon as they got back to Yellowstone Park, they found a park ranger and told him all about what had happened. "A car was stolen last night," the ranger told them. "That must be it." He called for more help and for a rescue truck. Very quickly, two ranger cars and the rescue truck were on their way to the wrecked car. Jeff and Rita rode with them.

Two Idaho state policemen were already checking out the wrecked Cobra. "What did you find?" the park ranger called as he pulled up by the Cobra. "Are the people still alive?"

"There's no one in the car," one of the state policemen said.

"There isn't?" Jeff asked as he jumped out of the ranger's car. "But there were two men in it! I saw them! We rode back to the park for help right away. It can't have been more than an hour since the car crashed."

"Well we got a call from a passing truck driver just before we got the call from the ranger. The truck driver didn't see anyone. He just told us about the car." The policeman looked hard at Jeff and went on, "So you saw the crash? Did you stop and try to help the people in the car?"

"No, I didn't dare!" Jeff told the policemen about how the Cobra had tried to run them off the road.

"And you don't know why?" the policeman asked.

"No! I'd never seen that car before in my life!"

"Well, we'll have to make a full report," the policeman said. "We'll need to know where we can reach you in California. Then you'll be free to go on."

It was afternoon by the time Jeff and Rita got back to Yellowstone Park to get their motorcycle. Soon they were on the road again. As they passed the wrecked car, they could see a truck getting ready to tow it away.

Jeff and Rita didn't stop. They roared on down the

highway as fast as they could. They just wanted to get through Idaho.

They knew that the men from the Cobra must be out there somewhere—somewhere near. Jeff and Rita wanted to put some miles between them.

Comprehension Questions*/Chapter 5*

Directions. Answer these questions about the chapter you have just read. Put an *x* in the box beside the best answer to each question.

1. (A) Jeff said, "I'll bet Mop woke up everyone in the campground last night. *What got into her, anyway?*" What did he mean?

   ☐ a. What made her do that?
   ☐ b. What had she been eating?
   ☐ c. What had she been planning?
   ☐ d. What bit her?

2. (E) What was the main thing that Rita and Jeff wanted to do in the first part of this chapter?

   ☐ a. Put Mop on the train
   ☐ b. Enjoy the sights of Yellowstone Park
   ☐ c. Leave Yellowstone Park as fast as they could
   ☐ d. Find the van

3. (E) Why did Ken and Steve want to kill Jeff and Rita?

   ☐ a. They were angry that Mop had got into the van.
   ☐ b. They didn't like people who rode motorcycles.
   ☐ c. They thought that Jeff and Rita were police who were following them.
   ☐ d. They thought that Jeff and Rita wanted to steal the van.

4. (D) How were the two men going to kill Jeff and Rita?

- ☐ a. By forcing them over the edge of a cliff
- ☐ b. By hitting them with the car
- ☐ c. By leaving them in the old barn
- ☐ d. By shooting at them from the car

5. (B) Where did Ken and Steve get the Cobra?

- ☐ a. They found it in an old barn.
- ☐ b. They got it from a park ranger.
- ☐ c. They stole it from someone at another campsite.
- ☐ d. They traded their van for it.

6. (A) Steve said, "We're crossing a state line in a stolen car. *We're getting into this deeper and deeper.*" What was he afraid of?

- ☐ a. They were sinking into the water.
- ☐ b. More and more people were following them.
- ☐ c. They were going to go over the cliff.
- ☐ d. They were breaking more and more laws.

7. (D) Think about how Steve went about getting the Cobra. What does this tell you about him?

- ☐ a. He was not very smart.
- ☐ b. He knew a lot about campgrounds.
- ☐ c. He was afraid of the dark.
- ☐ d. He had stolen cars before.

8. (C) What happened just before the Cobra skidded and rolled?

- ☐ a. Jeff looked in his mirror.
- ☐ b. Jeff turned the motorcycle in a U-turn.
- ☐ c. Jeff stopped the motorcycle by the side of the road.
- ☐ d. Jeff asked Rita if she was all right.

9. (C) Who were the first people to go and check on the wrecked car?

- ☐ a. Jeff and Rita
- ☐ b. The park rangers
- ☐ c. The state police
- ☐ d. The man who owned the Cobra

10. (B) Who told the state police about the wrecked car?

- ☐ a. Jeff and Rita
- ☐ b. Ken and Steve
- ☐ c. The man who owned the Cobra
- ☐ d. A truck driver who drove by it

Skills Used to Answer Questions

A. Recognizing Words in Context B. Recalling Facts
C. Keeping Events in Order D. Making Inferences
E. Understanding Main Ideas

Commas in Dates and Place Names

So far in this book you have learned how to use commas in four different ways:

1. In compound sentences
2. In a list of items
3. With quotations
4. In direct address

You know that a comma tells you to pause slightly in a sentence. Now you will learn two new ways to use commas: in dates and in place names.

Commas in Dates

Look at the dates printed below.

Monday, March 11
Monday, March 11, 1985

You can see that there are commas after each item in the date except for the last item. In both examples above, there is a comma between the day of the week and the day of the month—Monday, March 11. In the second example, there is also a comma between the day of the month and the year—March 11, 1985. Read the two sentences below. Each contains a date.

I began work at my new job on Monday, March 11, 1985.
Monday, March 11, 1985 was my first day of work.

When a date is given in a sentence, commas are placed after each item in the date except for the last item. The commas tell you to pause slightly.

Exercise 1

The following dates have been written without commas. On the lines provided, print the dates, filling in commas where they belong. The first one has been done for you as an example.

1. April 12 1963 April 12, 1963
2. Sunday April 12 1963 ______
3. Friday December 6 ______
4. June 6 1978 ______
5. Thursday May 30 1966 ______
6. November 14 1938 ______

Exercise 2

The following sentences with dates have no commas. Print each sentence on the lines provided, writing in commas where they belong. Remember that you should put a comma after each item in a date except for the last item. The first one has been done for you as an example.

1. My sister was born on Thursday July 1 1958.

   My sister was born on
   Thursday, July 1, 1958.

2. Monday June 13 is Janet's graduation day.

3. This year we will celebrate Martin Luther King's birthday on Monday January 15.

4. We moved to Texas on Friday May 22 1955.

5. Can you finish the job by Saturday April 11?

6. Wednesday July 4 is a holiday for the whole family.

Commas in Place Names

Look at the place names below.

> Vera Cruz, Mexico
> Michigan Avenue, Chicago, Illinois, United States of America

In the first example, there is a comma between the name of the city (Vera Cruz) and the name of the country (Mexico). In the second example, there are three commas. The first comma is placed between the street address (Michigan Avenue) and the city (Chicago). The second comma is placed between the city and the state (Chicago, Illinois). The third comma is placed between the name of the state and the name of the country (Illinois, United States of America). You can see that a comma is put after each item in a place name except for the last item. Read the sentences below. Each contains a place name. Notice where the commas are placed.

> I live at 85 Michigan Avenue, Chicago, Illinois.
> 85 Michigan Avenue, Chicago, Illinois is my home.

When a place name is given in a sentence, a comma is placed after each item in the place name except for the last item.

Exercise 3

The place names below have been written without commas. On the lines provided, print the place names, writing in commas where they belong. The first one has been done for you as an example.

1. Trafalgar Square London England

   Trafalgar Square, London, England

2. 14 Locust Street Burlington Vermont

3. Toronto Ontario

4. Grant Avenue San Francisco California United States of America

Exercise 4

The following sentences contain place names but no commas. Copy the sentences on the lines provided, writing in commas where they belong. Remember, a comma is put after each item in a place name except for the last item. The first one has been done for you as an example.

1. André lives in Paris France.

   André lives in Paris, France

2. Sally drove to Santa Fe New Mexico.

3. Have you ever been to London England?

4. Bogotá Colombia is a large city.

5. My address is 55 Blake Street Fort Wayne Indiana.

Total Cost: Part Two

The total cost of a mail order is the sum of three amounts:

1. The total price for items
2. The sales tax
3. The shipping charge

You already know how to figure the total price for items and the sales tax. Now you will learn how to figure the shipping charge.

Shipping Charge by Weight

When you buy items through the mail, you usually have to pay the cost of sending the order to your home or to a pick-up center near you. This cost is called a *shipping charge.* The amount of the shipping charge often depends on the *total weight of your order.* Look at the sample order on the right. The shopper is buying a sleeping bag, a flashlight, and a tent. She must pay a shipping charge based on the weight of her order.

The total weight of this order is 9.6 pounds (lbs.). It is the sum of the weights of the sleeping bag (3.2 lbs.), the tent (5.4 lbs.), and the flashlight (1 lb.). The figure 9.6 is entered in the box marked TOTAL WEIGHT at the bottom of the weight column.

Once you know the total weight of the order, you can figure the shipping charge. Use the shipping charge table printed in the catalog to find the amount you must pay for shipping and handling your order. Part of a shipping charge table is shown below the order form.

Item Information

PAGE NUMBER	NAME OF ITEM	CATALOG NUMBER letter	CATALOG NUMBER number	SIZE	COLOR (name & number)	HOW MANY	PRICE dollars	PRICE cents	WEIGHT
65	Sleeping bag	Z	496-31		green 43	1	40	00	3.2 lbs.
114	Tent	Z	643-11		blue 5	1	60	00	5.4 lbs.
123	Flashlight	Z	489-42		red 24	1	10	00	1.0 lb.
							110	00	9.6 lbs.

TOTAL PRICE FOR ITEMS — TOTAL WEIGHT

Order Totals

TOTAL PRICE FOR ITEMS	110	00
SALES TAX	4	40
SHIPPING AND HANDLING	1	96
TOTAL COST	116	36

WEIGHT	SHIPPING CHARGE
0 – .5 lb.	.86
.6 – 1 lb.	1.23
1.1 – 2 lbs.	1.52
2.1 – 3 lbs.	1.58
3.1 – 4 lbs.	1.64
4.1 – 5 lbs.	1.71
5.1 – 6 lbs.	1.77
6.1 – 7 lbs.	1.84
7.1 – 8 lbs.	1.89
8.1 – 9 lbs.	1.92
9.1 – 10 lbs.	1.96
10.1 – 11 lbs.	2.01
11.1 – 12 lbs.	2.05
12.1 – 13 lbs.	2.10
13.1 –14 lbs.	2.14

To find your shipping charge on a shipping charge table, follow these steps:

1. Look at the column marked WEIGHT. Find the weight line that includes the weight of your order. Notice that each line gives a *range* of rates. For example, the first line is for orders weighing *between* 0 and 5 pounds. The total weight of your order must be equal to or in between the two weights given on a line. On the sample order form on the last page, the total weight is 9.6 pounds. That is more than 9.1 pounds, but less than 10 pounds. The line *9.1-10 lbs.* is the correct weight line for the order.
2. Read across from the WEIGHT line to the SHIPPING CHARGE line beside it. The charge given to the right of the weight line for your order is the amount you must pay for shipping and handling. The shipping charge for the weight line *9.1-10 lbs.* is 1.96. The buyer must pay $1.96 to have the order sent to her home or to a pick-up center near her.
3. Enter the shipping charge in the box marked SHIPPING AND HANDLING on the order form.

Use the same table to answer the questions below. Suppose you order a picnic basket and a tablecloth through the mail. The total weight of your order is 13.8 pounds.

What is the correct weight line for your order? Copy that line here:

____

How much must you pay for shipping and handling? Print your answer here:

____

Shipping Charge by Price

You have just learned that some mail order companies base the charge for shipping and handling on the total weight of the order. Other companies base the shipping charge on the *total price for items*. Look at the order form below. The shopper is buying a wooden clothes dryer and a sled. He must pay a shipping charge based on the total price for the items he has ordered.

Item Information

PAGE NUMBER	NAME OF ITEM	CATALOG NUMBER		SIZE	COLOR	HOW MANY	PRICE		WEIGHT
		letter	number		(name & number)		dollars	cents	
18	Alpine sled		6281			1	62	00	
27	Wooden clothes dryer		4543			1	22	50	
							84	50	
							TOTAL PRICE FOR ITEMS		TOTAL WEIGHT

Charges for shipping, handling and insurance within the United States

Order Total	Shipping Charge
up to $15.00	$2.50
$15.01-$30.00	$3.00
$30.01-$50.00	$4.25
$50.01-$100.00	$5.25
over $100.00	$6.00

Order Totals

TOTAL PRICE FOR ITEMS	84	50
DELIVERY TO VERMONT ADDRESS, ADD 4% TAX		
SHIPPING, HANDLING AND INSURANCE	5	25
TOTAL COST		

The total price for the items ordered is $84.50. It is the sum of the price of the wooden clothes dryer ($22.50) and the price of the sled ($62.00). The figure 84.50 is entered in the box marked TOTAL PRICE FOR ITEMS.

Once you know the total price for items, you can figure the shipping charge. Use the table printed on the order form to find the amount you must pay for shipping and handling. The table is shown on the form above.

To find the shipping charge, follow these steps:

1. Look at the column marked *order total.* Find the price line for your order. The total price for items should be equal to or in between the two prices given on the line. On the sample order form on the last page, the total price for items is $84.50. That is more than $50.01 but less than $100.00. The line *$50.01-$100.00* is the correct price line for the order.
2. Read across from the correct price line to the *shipping charge* line beside it. The charge given to the right of the correct price line for your order is the amount you must pay for shipping and handling. The shipping charge for orders totaling between $50.01 and $100.00 is $5.25. That is what the buyer of the above order must pay.
3. Enter the shipping charge in the box marked SHIPPING AND HANDLING on the order form.

Suppose you ordered a handbag and a sweater from the same company. The total price for your items is $46.00. Use the shipping charge table above to answer these questions.

What is the correct price line for your order? Copy that line here:

____

How much must you pay for shipping and handling? Print your answer here:

____

Fixed Shipping Charges

You have learned that some mail order companies base the charge for shipping and handling on either the total weight or the total price for items. There are also companies that charge the same amount for shipping any order. It does not matter how much the order weighs or costs. A shipping charge that is always the same is called a *fixed shipping charge.*

If a shipping charge is fixed, it is printed right on the order form. Look at the order below.

Item Information

PAGE NUMBER	NAME OF ITEM	CATALOG NUMBER letter	CATALOG NUMBER number	SIZE	COLOR (name & number)	HOW MANY	PRICE dollars	PRICE cents	WEIGHT
25	Swiss army knife		6843190		red	1	20	00	
36	Day pack		4522931		navy	1	16	00	
						TOTAL PRICE FOR ITEMS	36	00	TOTAL WEIGHT:

Order Totals

TOTAL PRICE FOR ITEMS	36	00
FOR DELIVERY IN WISC. ADD 5% SALES TAX; IN ILL. 5%; IN IOWA 4%		
SHIPPING, PACKING, HANDLING AND INSURANCE	2	80
TOTAL COST		

You can see there is a fixed shipping charge of $2.80. That is the charge for any order. The shipping charge does not depend on weight or price. You do not have to write the weight of each item or the total weight on the order form. You do not have to use a table to find the shipping charge. You just pay the amount that is printed on the order form.

Finding the Shipping Charge

Mail order companies often make you pay the cost of shipping your order. Sometimes the shipping charge is based on the total weight or total price for items. Then you use a shipping charge table to find the shipping charge. Sometimes there is a fixed shipping charge. That means that you pay the same amount no matter what your order weighs or costs. The fixed charge is printed right on the order form. If the shipping charge is fixed, you do not have to figure the weight of the order.

Exercise 1

Part of a shipping charge table is shown below. The shipping charge is based on the total weight of the order.

WEIGHT	SHIPPING CHARGE
8.1 - 9 lbs.	1.92
9.1 - 10 lbs.	1.96
10.1 - 11 lbs.	2.01
11.1 - 12 lbs.	2.05
12.1 - 13 lbs.	2.10
13.1 - 14 lbs.	2.14
14.1 - 15 lbs.	2.19
15.1 - 16 lbs.	2.24
16.1 - 17 lbs.	2.30
17.1 - 18 lbs.	2.36
18.1 - 19 lbs.	2.42
19.1 - 20 lbs.	2.48
20.1 - 21 lbs.	2.54
21.1 - 22 lbs.	2.60
22.1 - 23 lbs.	2.65
23.1 - 24 lbs.	2.71
24.1 - 25 lbs.	2.77
25.1 - 26 lbs.	2.83
26.1 - 27 lbs.	2.89
27.1 - 28 lbs.	2.95
28.1 - 29 lbs.	3.01
29.1 - 30 lbs.	3.07
30.1 - 31 lbs.	3.13
31.1 - 32 lbs.	3.19
32.1 - 33 lbs.	3.24
33.1 - 34 lbs.	3.30
34.1 - 35 lbs.	3.36
35.1 - 36 lbs.	3.42
36.1 - 37 lbs.	3.48
37.1 - 38 lbs.	3.54

Use the table to find the shipping charges for each of the orders that follow. For each one, follow these steps:

1. Find the number in the box marked TOTAL WEIGHT on the order form.
2. Look at the shipping charge table. Find the weight line for the total weight of the order. The total weight should be between the two numbers given on the weight line.
3. Read across from the correct weight line to the SHIPPING CHARGE line beside it. The charge given to the right of the weight line is the shipping charge for the order.

Copy the correct weight line for each order on the first blank line. Print the shipping charge for each order on the second blank line. The first one has been done for you as an example.

1.

NAME OF ITEM	WEIGHT
Sewing machine	24.2
Carrying case	2.6
TOTAL WEIGHT	26.8

The weight line is 26.1 — 27 lbs. .

The shipping charge is $ 2.89 .

2.

NAME OF ITEM	WEIGHT
13-inch color TV	30.7
Veneer TV table	7.2
TOTAL WEIGHT	37.9

The weight line is ______________________ .

The shipping charge is ______________________ .

3.

NAME OF ITEM	WEIGHT
Plain-toe hiking boots	5.5
Plain-toe work boots	5.3
Oxford shoes	4.0
TOTAL WEIGHT	14.8

The weight line is ______________________ .

The shipping charge is ______________________ .

4.

NAME OF ITEM	WEIGHT
Set of 3 bath towels	2.6
Set of 6 washcloths	1.1
Set of 3 guest towels	1.4
Bathroom scale	6.0
	11.1

TOTAL WEIGHT

The weight line is ________________________ .

The shipping charge is ____________________ .

Exercise 2

A shipping charge table is shown below. For this company, the shipping charge is based on the total price for items.

Charges for shipping, handling and insurance within the United States

Order Total	Shipping Charge
up to $15.00:	$2.50
$15.01–$30.00:	$3.00
$30.01–$50.00:	$4.25
$50.01–$100.00:	$5.25
over $100.00:	$6.00

Use the table to find the shipping charge for each of the following orders. Follow these steps:

1. Find the total price for items. Remember that TOTAL FOR GOODS, ITEM TOTAL, and PRICE OF ITEMS all mean *total price for items.*
2. Look at the table. Find the price line for the total price for items. The total price for items should lie between the two figures on the price line.
3. Read across from the correct price line to the amount given beside it. The amount to the right of the correct price line is the shipping charge for the order.

Copy the correct price line for each order on the first blank line. Print the shipping charge for each order on the second blank line. The first one has been done for you as an example.

1.

NAME OF ITEM	PRICE	
	dollars	cents
Sewing machine	199	50
Carrying case	25	00
	224	50

TOTAL PRICE FOR ITEMS

The price line is over $100.00 .

The shipping charge is $6.00 .

2.

NAME OF ITEM	PRICE	
	dollars	cents
13-inch color TV	398	99
TV table	65	00
	463	99

TOTAL PRICE FOR ITEMS

The price line is ______________________ .

The shipping charge is ______________________ .

3.

NAME OF ITEM	PRICE	
	dollars	cents
Tennis shoes	33	00
Can of 3 tennis balls	2	89
Sweat socks	4	00
	39	89

TOTAL PRICE FOR ITEMS

The price line is ______________________ .

The shipping charge is ______________________ .

4.

NAME OF ITEM	PRICE	
	dollars	cents
Set of 3 bath towels	9	00
Set of 3 guest towels	6	00
Set of 6 washcloths	5	00
Bath mat	6	50
TOTAL PRICE FOR ITEMS	26	50

The price line is ______________________ .

The shipping charge is ______________________ .

6

The Last Move

Preview Words/*Chapter 6*

Study the words in the box. Then read the sentences below with your teacher. Look carefully at the words in boldface type.

acting	fault	motel	radio
beach	footsteps	newspapers	story
bridge	gulp	ocean	themselves
clinging	instead	pancakes	unless
coast	lady	puppies	waded

1. They didn't camp out. **Instead**, they looked for a place to stay.
2. They stayed in a **motel** in a big town.
3. It's a pain to make **pancakes** over a campfire.
4. He took a last **gulp** of coffee.
5. They found **themselves** thinking about the end of the trip.
6. You can't make a turn like that **unless** you've been trained how to do it.
7. They crossed over a big river on a **bridge**.
8. This way, we can get to the **ocean** by tomorrow.
9. Rita was **clinging** to the sissy bar.
10. She'll change her **story** soon.
11. You know what we're talking about, little **lady**.
12. She could hear their **footsteps** behind her.
13. "I know," Rita said. "It wasn't your **fault**."
14. I don't like the way you guys are **acting**.
15. You get into the truck and use my CB **radio**.
16. They parked the bike and walked to the **beach**.
17. They took off their boots and **waded** into the water.
18. They were riding down the **coast** of Oregon.
19. Our dog had six **puppies**, but we gave two away.
20. I'll bet the story was in all the **newspapers**.

Jeff and Rita felt better as they crossed Idaho. The highway swung south, out of the tall mountains. As the miles went quickly by, they began to forget about how the Cobra had tried to push them off the road. It all began to seem like just a bad dream.

Just to be safe, they didn't camp out that night. Instead, they stayed in a motel in a big town and had their breakfast in a restaurant nearby.

"These pancakes are good!" Jeff said. "It's nice to have breakfast in a restaurant for a change. It's a pain in the neck to make pancakes over a campfire."

"Yes, they are good," Rita said, "but I like being outdoors. And I feel bad when we can't let Mop come in with us," she added, looking out at Mop tied to the motorcycle in front of the motel. "She looks so sad out there all alone."

"Oh, she's all right!" Jeff said with his mouth full of pancakes. "How can you tell if she's sad or not? She's nothing but a ball of fur."

"Well her fur hangs down when she's sad."

"You and that dog!" Jeff said. "I can't believe it!" He took a last gulp of coffee. "I'm all done anyway. Let's go. You can take Mop for a walk while I pack up the bike."

They moved on across Idaho, with the highway rolling smoothly under their tires. They could feel that they had come a long, long way from New York. It wouldn't be much longer before they would be in California.

They found themselves thinking about the end of the trip. Jeff thought about going back to work. Rita thought about looking for a job. When they made rest stops, they talked about San Francisco. They spent more and more time thinking about where they would be in just two or three more days, and less and less time thinking about the wrecked Cobra.

But Ken and Steve had not forgotten about them. And they were not as far behind them as Jeff and Rita thought.

* * * * *

When the Cobra crashed, Ken and Steve had been lucky—and smart. After the crash, they waited until Rita and Jeff were out of sight, on their way back to Yellowstone Park to get help. Then the two men pulled themselves out of the wrecked car. They were not badly hurt, but they were banged up and mad.

"Did you see the way that guy could make that bike move?" Steve growled. "You can't make a turn like that unless you've been trained how to do it. They're cops all right."

"I'll get them if it's the last thing I do!" Ken said. "But they've gone for help. We've got to get out of here!"

They walked on down the road and around the bend, and they waited. Soon a truck came along and stopped. "Where are you headed?" the truck driver asked.

"We're going east, through Yellowstone Park and into Wyoming."

"Well I'm going right across Wyoming, so hop in." The truck moved on up the mountain, back the way they had come. Soon they were passing the wrecked Cobra. "Wow! That's some wreck!" the truck driver said.

"I'll say! There doesn't seem to be anyone in it," Ken said.

"It must have happened a while back," the truck driver said, "but just in case, I'll call in on my CB radio. The state police can come out and have a look."

"Sounds good," Steve said. He and Ken just sat back and watched the road go by.

Soon they were through Yellowstone Park and headed for the town where they had hidden the van. When they got to the town, they got out of the truck. They had lunch in a restaurant, then spent the afternoon in a pool hall.

As soon as it got dark, they walked out to the old barn. The van was waiting for them, just as they had left it. A moment later they were on the road again, headed west.

* * * * *

Jeff and Rita had crossed Idaho. Now they were crossing over a big river. In the middle of the bridge, they passed another state sign:

WELCOME TO OREGON

On the other side of the river, Jeff pulled off the road and got a road map out of the saddlebag. "We're getting off the main highway now," he said. "There won't be as many cars around, and this way is much shorter. We can get to the ocean by tomorrow."

"That sounds great!" Rita said. "I can't wait to see the Pacific Ocean."

"You're not worried about those men in that car?" Jeff asked.

"Oh no," Rita said. "They're way back east, on the other side of Idaho."

"OK." Jeff turned off the highway and followed Route 20 due west.

It was only an hour later that Ken and Steve reached the river in the van. They had been driving all night and all day, and they were tired. But anger and fear pushed them on.

Ken was looking at the map. "Get off the main

highway here. Route 20 is much faster. It goes straight across the state. Then we'll cut down on this road, into California. We'll pick up the highway again here," he said, poking a finger hard into the map. "We'll be in San Francisco tomorrow."

"What about those cops on the motorcycle?" Steve asked.

"We'll see them again. I can feel it in my bones," Ken told him. "We'll get them."

Steve pulled out onto Route 20, headed west across Oregon.

* * * * *

Rita and Jeff were making good time. The land was dry, and they were out of the mountains. They saw hardly any cars on the road. They pushed on, thinking about California.

Suddenly, POW! The motorcycle swung around, spinning right across the road. They were going down! Jeff pulled his leg up fast, climbing up the motorcycle as it went down. "Don't lean! Climb!" he yelled to Rita.

The motorcycle skidded across the pavement. When it came to a stop at last, Jeff turned quickly and asked, "Rita! Are you all right?"

Rita was clinging to the sissy bar, with her feet up on the seat. "I'm all right," she said. "I just did what I saw you do. I climbed up as it went over. Are you all right? Is Mop all right?"

"I'm OK. And, yes, your darned dog is OK too." They climbed off the motorcycle and pulled it over to the side of the road. "Just what I thought, a blowout," Jeff said. "We must have worn the tires down making all those turns to get away from that car."

Rita asked, "Can you fix a blowout?"

"Not by myself," Jeff said. "I'll have to take the tire in to a garage."

Just then an old car came down the road. It stopped, and an old man leaned out the window and asked, "Having trouble?"

"We had a blowout," Jeff told him.

"Is there anything I can do to help?" the old man asked. "You don't carry a spare tire on those things, do you?"

"No, but could you take us into the nearest town?" Jeff asked. "I can take the rear wheel right off and put it in the trunk of your car."

"Sounds fine to me," the man said. "But are you just going to leave the motorcycle there? It might not be there when you get back."

"You're right," Jeff said. He looked around. What were they going to do?

"You go into town," Rita said. "I'll stay with the bike."

"Are you sure you'll be all right?" Jeff asked.

"Of course I will. It's almost supper time, anyway. We can camp right here. I'll put up the tent and start our supper while I'm waiting for you. Don't worry," she laughed, "I'll have Mop to take care of me."

"OK." Jeff quickly took the rear wheel off the motorcycle and loaded it into the trunk of the old man's car. "I'll be back as soon as I can," he said, giving Rita a kiss. Then he was gone.

Rita got the tent out of the saddlebag of the motorcycle. She found a nice flat spot, back a little from the road, and set up the tent. Then she got out the sleeping bags and spread them out in the tent.

She spent some time playing with Mop, running

up and down in the grass by the side of the road. When it was time to start supper, she headed for the motorcycle to get the food out of the saddlebag. Mop ran beside her, barking for food.

Just then a van pulled up.

Two men got out.

Rita looked up from the saddlebag. "I don't need any help, thank you," she told the two men. "My husband has gone to get the tire fixed. He'll be right back."

"You're a cool one," Steve said. "Look at her," he told Ken. "She has her story all ready. She doesn't even bat an eye."

Ken nodded. "She'll change her story soon," he said. "Just watch."

Rita took a step back. "What are you talking about?" she asked. Mop had just been sitting and waiting for supper, but now she started to growl. It was such a tiny sound that the men didn't even hear it.

Ken and Steve walked slowly toward Rita. "You know what we're talking about, little lady," Ken said. "You've been following us all the way across the country."

"No, I . . ." Rita quickly stepped in back of the motorcycle. She looked around for something to throw at them. "I didn't . . ."

"What's the matter?" Ken laughed. "Is your gun in your tent?"

"My gun? I . . . Yes, my gun! It's right here!" She grabbed her helmet and threw it as hard as she could at Ken. He jumped quickly out of the way. She reached for Jeff's helmet, but Steve ran toward her. Ken was coming at her from the other side. She ran, gasping with fear.

She could hear their footsteps behind her. They were getting closer! She ran out across the dry grasslands.

There was nowhere to hide.

Steve was very close behind her. He grabbed for her hair, but she pulled away and kept running. Then suddenly he jumped and grabbed her around the legs, and she went down hard in the dirt. In a moment, Steve had grabbed her arm. He twisted it tightly around her back and made her get up. Still holding her arm behind her back, he pushed her toward the road again.

Mop ran beside them, growling as loudly as she could. She tried to bite Steve's leg, but Steve just kicked her away. "Get out of here, dog!" he said. "Get out of here or I'll mop up the road with you!" He dragged Rita over to the van. "What are we going to do with her?" he asked Ken.

"We have to get rid of her," Ken said. "She knows too much. It's bad enough that she knows about the paintings, but they could get us for trying to kill them back there with the Cobra."

"The Cobra!" Rita said. "You were in that Cobra? You tried to kill us! But why? I don't know about any paintings!"

Ken laughed a cold laugh. "You can't pull that on us, little lady. We heard you talking about the paintings, the museum—everything!"

Rita's mouth fell open. "The museum . . . You're the ones who broke into the museum! And you think we've been following you?"

"We *know* you've been following us!" Ken opened the back of the van. "You wanted the paintings? Well there they are. Now you can see them real close—until we get rid of you. Get in!"

Steve pushed Rita toward the open van. "No, no!" Rita shouted, fighting to get free. Mop bit at Steve's legs, growling. She bit into his pants leg and held on, but Steve just walked on, dragging the little dog through the dirt.

Now they were almost at the van. Suddenly they heard something coming. A truck! A big truck was coming along the road. Rita made one last try to twist away from Steve, but he held her tightly. "If you try to wave to that truck," he said, "it will be the last thing you ever do."

The truck came toward them along the long, flat road. Ken tried to look as if he was fixing the motorcycle. Steve kept a tight hold on Rita. Rita just looked at the truck. It was her last chance—but the driver wasn't even looking at them. He would just drive on by and never know how much she needed him. If only he would look . . .

Suddenly Mop ran out into the road, right in front of the big truck. The driver hit the air brakes and tried to turn, but one of the huge front wheels took Mop and sent her flying through the air. "Mop!" Rita screamed. She tried to run to her dog, but Steve held her back.

"Don't move," Ken growled. "The dog got what was coming to it."

The truck pulled over and stopped. The driver got out and walked slowly back to where Mop was lying. He picked up the little dog and carried her to Rita and the two men. "It's dead," he said. "I'm sorry, I'm really sorry. I didn't know the dog would run out in front of me like that. I just couldn't stop in time."

"I know," Rita said through her tears. "It wasn't your fault."

The truck driver held Mop's body out to Rita, but Rita didn't reach out to take it. The truck driver looked at Rita for a long moment. Then he looked at Ken and Steve. At last he laid Mop's body down on the grass by Rita's feet and walked back to the truck.

Rita watched him go. Mop tried, she thought. Mop gave her life to stop that truck. And now he's going away.

The driver got into the truck, but he didn't shut the door. A moment later he climbed down again.

He had a gun in his hands.

He walked slowly toward Rita and the two men. "There's something going on here," he said. "I don't like the way you guys are acting toward the lady here. It looks to me as if you're holding her pretty tight." He waved the gun at Steve. "I think you'd better let go of her." Steve let go of Rita and backed up. The truck driver waved his gun at Ken, and Ken walked over to stand next to Steve. "OK," the truck driver said, "what's going on here? Are you all right?" he asked Rita.

"Yes, I'm OK," Rita said, rubbing her arms. "These men stole some paintings from a museum in New York City. The paintings are in the van. They thought my husband and I were following them. When our motorcycle blew a tire, they found me here alone. They said I knew too much, but I just know about the museum because my mother works there! So they were going to kill me. But Mop . . . my little dog . . ." Rita broke into tears again.

"It looks as if that little dog saved your life," the truck driver said. "Now you get into the truck and use my CB radio. Call anyone who hears you and tell them we need some help here."

Rita climbed into the truck and looked at the CB radio. How did it work? She picked up the mike and pushed buttons until she got it going. "Hello, everyone," she began. "I need help. Two robbers from New York City are here, and . . ." She stopped. She couldn't tell the whole story on the radio! "Hello? Hello?" She began again. "Please help me. I am on Route 20, an hour west of the Idaho state line. Please send the police. Please help me." She said it over and over. Was she getting through?

Just then a truck came down the road. It pulled over, and the driver jumped out and ran up to them. Soon another truck came, and a car. A man got up into the truck with Rita and showed her how to set the CB so that she could hear other people. More cars and trucks came, but Rita went on calling for help. Where were the police?

Suddenly a voice came over the CB calling, "Rita! Rita! Is that you? Are you all right?"

"Oh, Jeff! Yes, it's me! Those men, the ones who stole

the paintings . . . Oh, Jeff, Mop is dead!"

"Rita, hang on! We'll be there soon!"

A state police car pulled up, and two policemen jumped out. Rita got out of the truck and went over to them. "What's going on here?" the policemen were asking. "Who called for us?"

"I did," Rita told them. "I can tell you all about it." She told them the whole story and showed them the paintings in the van.

Just as she was done, a pickup truck pulled up and Jeff jumped out. He ran through the crowd of people looking for Rita. "Rita! Rita, what happened? Are you all right?" he asked as he threw his arms around her and held her tight. "I shouldn't have left you alone."

"I wasn't alone," Rita said. "I had Mop."

* * * * *

That night they stayed at a motel nearby. The next

morning they pushed on.

They rode west until they got to the Pacific Ocean. When they got their first sight of it, Rita gasped. It was so huge, and so blue.

They parked the motorcycle in a rest area and walked down to the beach. The beach was wide and flat, with big rocks here and there. "It doesn't look like the beaches back home," Rita said. "It doesn't look like the Atlantic Ocean at all." She looked out over the water for a moment, then looked back over the land. "From the Atlantic Ocean to the Pacific Ocean, right across the United States. We made it." She tried to sound happy, but she felt very sad.

They took off their boots and waded out into the water, hand in hand.

* * * * *

Now they were riding down the coast of Oregon. The road went right along the ocean, and they stopped often to look at the water. It was so pretty there. In the night, when the fog came rolling in off the water, even the fog was pretty.

The next day, as they rode on south, they crossed another state line. The sign said

WELCOME TO CALIFORNIA

California at last! Jeff pulled over to the side of the road and gave Rita a big hug. "The last day of our trip," he said. "Tomorrow we'll be in San Francisco."

"I feel a little sad about it," Rita said. "I don't want the trip to end. And now it won't feel right, going to San Francisco. Not without Mop."

"You know," Jeff said, "I miss her too. It seems strange to ride along without her in my jacket. But we can get another dog."

"It wouldn't be Mop," Rita said.

They camped that night in a park. Rita lit their last campfire, and Jeff cooked a big supper. They were just sitting down to eat when a camping trailer pulled in and stopped at the campsite next to them. The door opened and a big family spilled out until there were children everywhere. And there were dogs—little dogs that looked like dust mops.

"Oh look, Jeff!" Rita shouted, jumping up. "Look! They have a lot of little dogs, and they all look just like Mop!" Rita had forgotten all about her supper. She walked slowly toward the next campsite, watching the little dogs. She never took her eyes off them. Jeff got up and followed her.

A woman got out of the camping trailer. "Hello," she called to Rita. "We've got quite a gang here, don't we?"

"I was just looking at your dogs," Rita said softly. "I had a little dog just like them, but she was . . . hit by a truck."

"Oh, that's too bad," the woman said. She looked around her and added, "They *do* run around, don't they? That's the mother over there. She had six puppies, but we gave two away."

"Are you . . . Are you going to give any more away?" Rita asked.

"Oh, yes, we have to give them all away. Would you like one?" The woman looked over at Rita and Jeff's campsite. "Oh, you're on a motorcycle. That's too bad. You wouldn't have any place to put one. Floppy!" she shouted suddenly, running toward the motorcycle. "Get out of there!"

Rita and Jeff hurried after her. One of the puppies was up on the motorcycle, climbing into the open saddlebag. The woman grabbed the puppy and held it in her arms. "I'm sorry," she said, "but Floppy is always getting inside things."

Jeff and Rita looked at each other. Without saying anything, Jeff put on his big jacket. He took the puppy from the woman and tucked it down inside the jacket, where it curled up happily.

"I think we've picked one," Rita told the woman.

The next morning Jeff and Rita packed up the motorcycle for the last time. Floppy hopped into Jeff's jacket and curled up. They were ready to go.

"I just thought of something," Rita said. "Those robbers! When the police took them in, I'll bet the story was in all the newspapers!"

"Did you want to read about it?" Jeff asked. "I thought you wanted to forget all about it."

"I did. But my mother must have read all about it, and I forgot to call her! She must be very worried."

"You can call her tonight," Jeff said, "from home."

"From home. That sounds nice. Well, I hope my mother *did* read about it, so she'll know that Mop saved my life. She'll know what a good dog Mop was." Rita patted Floppy and added, "And I can tell her about our new puppy."

"Let's go," Jeff said. "San Francisco, here we come."

Comprehension Questions/*Chapter 6*

Directions. Answer these questions about the chapter you have just read. Put an *x* in the box beside the best answer to each question.

1. (B) How did Ken and Steve get away from the Cobra after the wreck?

   - ☐ a. A state police car picked them up.
   - ☐ b. They got a ride in a truck.
   - ☐ c. They walked back to Yellowstone Park.
   - ☐ d. They had the van hidden right nearby.

2. (A) Ken and Steve had been driving all night and all day, and they were tired. But *anger and fear pushed them on.* What does this mean?

   - ☐ a. They were afraid of Jeff and Rita's anger.
   - ☐ b. They kept on going because they were afraid and angry.
   - ☐ c. The police would not let them stop.
   - ☐ d. They got a push from someone at the garage.

3. (B) How did Jeff and Rita keep from getting hurt when the motorcycle had a blowout?

   - ☐ a. They jumped off.
   - ☐ b. They yelled for help.
   - ☐ c. They had their boots and helmets on.
   - ☐ d. They climbed up on it as it tipped over.

4. (E) Why did Jeff leave Rita alone with the motorcycle?

- ☐ a. He was so mad at Mop that he took her to the train.
- ☐ b. He was so mad at Rita that he flew the rest of the way to San Francisco.
- ☐ c. He had to go to town to get some food for supper.
- ☐ d. He had to take the tire to be fixed after the blowout.

5. (C) What happened next after Mop ran out in front of the truck?

- ☐ a. Steve grabbed Rita.
- ☐ b. Rita used the CB radio.
- ☐ c. The truck driver went over to talk to Rita.
- ☐ d. The truck driver got his gun.

6. (D) How did the truck driver know that Steve and Ken were holding Rita against her will?

- ☐ a. Rita did not take Mop's body when he held it out to her.
- ☐ b. Rita told him that Ken had a gun.
- ☐ c. He saw Rita trying to run away from them.
- ☐ d. He heard Rita calling for help on her CB radio.

7. (C) When did Jeff learn that Rita was in trouble?

- ☐ a. When he saw Ken and Steve chasing her
- ☐ b. When the police told him
- ☐ c. When he heard her voice on the CB radio
- ☐ d. When he saw the crowd of people around the motorcycle

8. (E) What thought did both Jeff and Rita have when they reached the Pacific Ocean?

- ☐ a. They could cool off on a hot day.
- ☐ b. They had gone all the way across the country.
- ☐ c. They were just glad to be in Oregon.
- ☐ d. They had got away from the men in the van.

9. (A) A camping trailer pulled into the next campsite. The door opened and a big family *spilled out.* What does this mean?

- ☐ a. Many people hurried out at once.
- ☐ b. Everyone fell out of the trailer.
- ☐ c. Many children pushed the door open.
- ☐ d. The family turned the trailer over.

10. (D) Why did Rita and Jeff pick out Floppy to be their new puppy?

- ☐ a. They knew that Floppy wouldn't make them think of Mop.
- ☐ b. They knew that Floppy could ride with them the way Mop had.
- ☐ c. The family had only one puppy left.
- ☐ d. Floppy was the only puppy that looked like Mop.

Skills Used to Answer Questions

A. Recognizing Words in Context B. Recalling Facts
C. Keeping Events in Order D. Making Inferences
E. Understanding Main Ideas

Review of Commas

You know that a comma is a punctuation mark that tells you to pause in a sentence. In this book you have learned six different uses for commas. Those six reasons for using commas are listed in the box below.

1. **Compound Sentence**
   Example: You take the chair, and I will take the lamp.
2. **List of Items**
   Example: I am bringing my ball, my bat, and my catcher's mitt to the game.
3. **Quotation**
   Example: "I like to play ball," said Jim.
4. **Direct Address**
   Example: Ed, call me when you get home.
5. **Date**
   Example: My sister took her first plane ride on Sunday, May 2, 1950.
6. **Place Name**
   Example: She flew to Lima, Peru.

Exercise 1

Read the sentences below. They all contain commas. Why are commas used in each of the sentences? Write the reason on the line below the sentence. Remember the six reasons you have learned for using commas. The first one has been done for you as an example.

1. Duluth, Minnesota gets cold in the winter.

   Place Name
   ____

2. Return the book by Thursday, June 10.

   ____

3. Would you like coffee, tea, or milk?

   ____

4. Keep your coat on, Manuel.

   ____

5. My favorite city is Phoenix, Arizona.

   ____

6. Ken is reading, but Al is watching TV.

   ____

7. "Let's go swimming," said Leon.

   ____

8. We bought a new stove, but our toaster is used.

   ____

Exercise 2

The sentences below have no commas. Copy the sentences on the lines provided, putting in commas where they belong. Then, in the box below each sentence, print the reason that you need the comma. The six reasons for using commas that you have learned are:

compound sentence	**direct address**
list of items	**date**
quotation	**place name**

The first one has been done for you as an example.

1. We bring pencils paper and books to class.

   We bring pencils, paper, and books to class.

   list of items

2. When will you come Wendy?

3. Marcia said "I like pizza."

4. I leave for Africa on Thursday July 2.

5. We need candy soda ice cream and cake for the party.

6. My son is six years old and my daughter is five.

7. Cindy comes from Boise Idaho.

8. Help me pack Fred.

The Final Order

To place a mail order with a company, you must follow these steps:

1. Fill in shopper information and item information on the order form.
2. Figure the total cost of your order. Enter the total for items, the sales tax, the shipping charge, and the total cost on the order form.
3. Choose a method of payment. Mark the method of payment on the order form.
4. Give your order to the company.

You already know how to fill out the order form and figure total cost. Now you will learn how to choose a method of payment. You will also learn how to give your order to the company.

Method of Payment

There are two ways to pay for a mail order. You can mail a check or money order with the order form, or you can use a credit card. The way you pay for your order is called the *method of payment.*

There is a method of payment section on order forms. It looks like this:

☑ **Check Method of Payment**

☐ **I have enclosed a check or money order.**

☐ **Charge to my:** master charge THE INTERBANK CARD VISA
(Circle one)

Card #: ☐☐☐☐☐☐☐☐☐☐☐☐☐☐☐☐

Expiration date: ☐☐ ☐☐

Signature (as shown on credit card)

Suppose you want to pay for an order by check or by money order. You should follow these steps:

1. Put a check mark in the box next to the statement *I have enclosed a check or money order.*
2. Write a check or money order for the amount of the total cost of your order. You can buy a money order for the exact amount at the bank or post office. A money order is used like a check. The check or money order should be made out to the company.
3. Send the check or money order together with your order form to the company.

Suppose you wanted to charge your order to a credit card. You would follow these steps:

1. Put a check mark in the box next to the words *Charge to my.*
2. Circle the the credit card to which you are charging your order. (You can charge your order only to one of the credit cards listed).
3. Print your credit card number in the space provided.
4. Print the *Expiration date* of your credit card in the space provided. The expiration date is the month and year in which you will need a new card. The expiration date is shown on the front of your card.
5. Sign your name on the line marked *Signature (as shown on credit card).*
6. Send the completed order form to the company.

Orders by Mail

There are two ways to get a mail order to a company. You can send your order through the mail, or you can telephone your order to the company.

Suppose you wanted to send your order through the mail. You would follow these steps:

1. Check the catalog entry and your order form to make sure all the item information is correct.
2. Check your order form to make sure the total price for items, sales tax, shipping charge, and total cost are figured and entered correctly.
3. Enclose a check or money order for the amount of the total cost, or enter the credit card information on the order form.
4. Send the completed order form to the company at the address given in the catalog.

Sometimes you will be placing an order with a small company that has only one mailing address. But sometimes you will be placing an order with a big national company that has several mailing addresses. If you are buying from a big company, the address to which you should send your order depends on where you live. There is an address table printed in the catalog to tell you where to send your order. Part of an address table from a J. C. Penney catalog is shown on the next page.

STATE	MAIL ORDER TO:
Oklahoma	J. C. Penney Catalog Division P.O. Box 2985 Shawnee Mission, Kansas 66250
Oregon	J. C. Penney Catalog Division P.O. Box 6231 Reno, Nevada 89599
Pennsylvania	J. C. Penney, Inc. Catalog Division Manchester, Connecticut 06041
Rhode Island	J. C. Penney, Inc. Catalog Division Manchester, Connecticut 06041
South Carolina	J. C. Penney, Inc. 90 Annex Atlanta, Georgia 30390
South Dakota	J. C. Penney Catalog Division P.O. Box 2985 Shawnee Mission, Kansas 66250

To use the table, find the state where you live in the column marked STATE. The states are listed in alphabetical order. The address to which you should send your order is given to the right of the state name, in a column marked MAIL ORDER TO. For example, if you lived in Pennsylvania, you would mail your order to J.C. Penney, Inc., Catalog Division, Manchester, Connecticut 06041.

Where would you send your order if you lived in Oregon? Print your answer in the space provided.

____

____

____

Orders by Phone

If you want to telephone an order to a company, follow these steps.

1. Find the phone number of the company's store or outlet nearest you. (You can find the number by looking under the company's name in the phone book. The phone number may also be given on the order form.)
2. Check the catalog entry and your order form to make sure that all item information is correct. You will have to read the item information over the phone.
3. Check your order form to make sure you have correctly figured and entered the total price for items, sales tax, shipping charge, and total cost. You should tell the company how much you expect to pay for your order. If you cannot figure the sales tax or total cost for yourself, ask the person on the phone to help you do it.
4. Give your credit card number and expiration date. Usually, you charge your order to a credit card when you order by phone.

When you finish speaking on the phone, your order is in.

Mail or Phone?

Should you order by mail or by phone? The answer is up to you. If you order by phone, you can get some help in figuring out sales tax and total cost. But you will probably have to use a credit card to place your order. The good thing about ordering by phone is that you usually get your order a little sooner. Either ordering method will get your order to you.

Placing Your Order

You have learned that you can place your order either by mail or by phone. You can pay for it by check or money order, or by charging it to your credit card. Whatever you do, be sure you have filled out the order form correctly. If you have, then the company will send you the right items. Also, you will know exactly how much you must pay for your order, including sales tax and shipping charge.

Exercise 1

Suppose you decide to use your VISA card to pay for a mail order. Your card number is 5141 102 881 375. The expiration date is 8/92 (August 1992). Use this information to fill out the *method of payment* section of the order form below. Sign the form with your own name. Your signature should match the name on your credit card.

☑ Check Method of Payment

☐ **I have enclosed a check or money order.**

☐ **Charge to my:** master charge THE INTERBANK CARD VISA
(Circle one)

Card #:

Expiration date:

Signature (as shown on credit card)

Exercise 2

The shoppers in this exercise have all decided to send their catalog orders through the mail. Use the address table below to find out where each shopper should send his or her order.

STATE	MAIL ORDER TO:
Tennessee	Sears Catalog Center Memphis, TN 38140
Texas	Sears Catalog Center Dallas, TX 75295
Utah	Sears Catalog Center Los Angeles, CA 90051
Vermont	Sears Catalog Center Boston, MA 02215
Virginia	Sears Catalog Center Philadelphia, PA 19138
Washington	Sears Catalog Center Seattle, WA 98184
West Virginia	Sears Catalog Center Greensboro, NC 27480
Wisconsin	Sears Catalog Center Chicago, IL 60607

Remember that the address to which an order from a large, national company should be sent depends on where the shopper lives. Write the correct address for each shopper in the space provided. The first one has been done for you as an example.

1. The shopper lives in Vermont.

   Sears Catalog Center
   Boston, MA 02215

2. The shopper lives in Washington.

   ____

   ____

3. The shopper lives in Utah.

   ____

   ____

4. The shopper lives in Tennessee.

   ____

   ____

5. The shopper lives in Wisconsin.

   ____

   ____

Exercise 3

Look at the completed order form below.

ORDER FORM

Shopper Information

AREA CODE ( ) HOME PHONE NUMBER	
NAME (first, middle initial, last)	
ADDRESS	
CITY/STATE	ZIP CODE

☑ Check Method of Payment

☐ I have enclosed a check or money order.

☑ Charge to my: (Circle one) master charge VISA

Card #: 6 1 8 5 2 0 3 4 6 5 1

Expiration date: 4 89

Francis R. Lombardo

Signature (as shown on credit card)

Item Information

PAGE NUMBER	NAME OF ITEM	CATALOG NUMBER letter	CATALOG NUMBER number	SIZE	COLOR (name & number)	HOW MANY	PRICE dollars	PRICE cents	WEIGHT
130	Striped sweater	Z	271-31	Large	gray/pink 80	1	27	00	1.6

TOTAL PRICE FOR ITEMS: 27 00 TOTAL WEIGHT: 1.6

Order Totals

TOTAL PRICE FOR ITEMS	27	00
SALES TAX	1	35
SHIPPING AND HANDLING	1	23
TOTAL COST	29	58

Suppose you have filled out this order form. You are placing your order by phone. On the phone, you will have to answer eight questions about your order. Use the information on the order form to answer each of the following questions. Print your answers in the spaces provided.

1. What is the page number of the catalog entry?

____

2. What is the name of the item? ______________

____

3. What size do you want? ______________

4. What color do you want? (Give name and number.)

____

5. What is the catalog number of the item?

____

6. How much does the item cost? ______________

7. What do you expect the total cost of your order to be?

____

8. What is your credit card number?

____

To the Instructor

Purpose of the Series

Teachers charged with the responsibility of providing instruction for adults and older students with reading difficulties face a major problem: the lack of suitable materials. Stories written at the appropriate level of maturity are too difficult; stories easy enough to read independently are too childish.

The stories in the Adult Learner Series were written to solve the readability problem. The plots and characters in these stories are suitable for adults and older students, yet the stories can be read easily by very low-level readers.

The principal goal of the series is to provide interest and enjoyment for these readers. To this end, every attempt has been made to creat a pleasant reading experience and to avoid frustration. The plots move quickly but are kept simple; a few characters are introduced and developed slowly; the same characters are utilized throughout a text; sentence structure and vocabulary are carefully monitored.

A secondary goal is to help adults explore and develop everyday life skills. Lessons and exercises about a variety of life skills provide adults and older students with the basic competencies they need for success in this fast-paced world.

Rounding out the structure of the series are exercises for developing vocabulary skills, comprehension skills, and language skills.

Reading Level

The stories in the Adult Learner Series are all written at the second and third grade reading levels. The first six titles in the series range from mid-first to second grade level; the next three titles are at the high-second and third grade levels. It should be kept in mind, however, that the stories were written for adults: people with a wider range of experience and larger speaking and listening vocabularies than those of elementary school children. Thus, there are some words and some events which might present difficulties for elementary school students but which should not pose problems for older beginning readers.

Besides the slightly increased complexity of vocabulary and plot, the writing style itself has been adapted for older beginning readers. Every effort was made to make the prose sound natural while maintaining simplicity of structure and vocabulary. The repetition of words and phrases has been carefully controlled to permit maximum learning of new words without producing a childish effect.

The reading levels of the stories were established by applying Dr. Edward B. Fry's *Formula for Estimating Readability* and *3,000 Instant Words* by Elizabeth Sakiey and Edward Fry. *3,000 Instant Words* lists the 3,000 most common words in the English language, ranked in order of frequency. The first 100 words on the list and their common variants [*-s, -ing,* etc.] make up 50 percent of all written material. The first 300 words and their variants make up 65 percent of all written material. Because readers encounter a relatively small number of words so frequently, they must be able to recognize the Instant Words immediately to be effective readers.

The story line of *Peril on the Road* presents some

concepts (camping, a rodeo) and places (the Badlands and the Grand Canyon) that may be new to some students. For them, and perhaps for all students, a discussion of these concepts might improve comprehension and enhance the element of reading for pleasure which is the primary purpose of all the stories in the Adult Learner Series.

Structure and Use of the Text

Each book in the Adult Learner Series is divided into several units. Each unit follows a regular format consisting of these sections:

Preview Words

Twenty words from each chapter are presented for students to preview before reading. Those words that were expected to give students the most difficulty were chosen for previewing. The preview section includes all words of more than one syllable that are not among the first 2,000 words on Sakiey and Fry's list of 3,000 Instant Words. The words are listed first in alphabetical order and then shown again in story sequence in sentences based on the chapter.

The twenty sentences match the chapter in readability; students can read the sentences independently. With some classes the instructor may want to read the words and sentences aloud for students to repeat and learn. In very structured classes, the words could also be used for spelling and writing practice.

Story

The primary purpose of the story is to provide interesting material for adult readers. It should be read as a story; the element of pleasure should be present. Because of the second grade reading level, students should be able to read the story on their own.

Comprehension Questions

Ten multiple-choice comprehension questions follow each chapter. There are two questions for each of these five comprehension skills:

A. Recognizing Words in Context
B. Recalling Facts
C. Keeping Events in Order
D. Making Inferences
E. Understanding Main Ideas

The letters *A* through *E* appear in the text as labels to identify the questions.

The comprehension questions are constructed to cover all parts of the chapter evenly and to bring out important points in the story. This insures that the student understands the story so far before going on to the next chapter.

Students should answer the questions immediately after reading the chapter and correct their answers using the key at the back of the book. Students should circle incorrect responses and check off correct ones.

The graphs at the back of the book help the instructor keep track of each student's comprehension progress. The *Comprehension Progress Graph* shows comprehension percentage scores. The *Skills Profile Graph* identifies areas of comprehension weakness needing special attention and extra practice.

Language Skills

These sections cover many aspects of language study:

phonics, word attack skills, simple grammar, spelling rules, punctuation and correct usage. The readability of these sections is higher than that of the chapters. The readability level varies depending on the vocabulary load of the specific language skill being taught.

Because the language skills are taught in clear and simple terms, most students will be able to work these sections independently. However, the instructor should be alert for opportunities to explain and further illustrate the content of the lessons.

The lessons contain exercises which give students the opportunity to practice the language skills being taught. An answer key at the back of the book makes it possible for students to correct their work.

Understanding Life Skills

Every chapter is accompanied by two sections which deal with life skills. The first, "Understanding Life Skills," introduces and fully explains a specific life skill. The life skills all revolve around some detail of modern adult life.

Because this section stresses *understanding* a certain life skill, the reading level is higher than the reading level of the story. However, the life skill lessons are presented in carefully prepared steps, and most students should be able to read and comprehend them without too much difficulty.

Questions used in the lessons are designed to focus the students' attention and to reinforce the learning. Answers for all questions are provided at the back of the book.

Applying Life Skills

Because modern-day living requires both *knowing*

and *doing,* two life skills sections follow each chapter to emphasize both aspects. The second, "Applying Life Skills," is primarily a practical exercise.

This section builds on the understanding generated in the previous section. Students should be able to complete the exercise successfully by applying what they have just read.

Completing this section allows students to demonstrate their mastery of a specific life skill. It gives them the firsthand experience they need with tasks they are likely to encounter in everyday living.

An Answer Key at the back of the book helps students correct their work and gives them immediate feedback.

All units in each book are structured alike, each consisting of the six sections described here. Students quickly discover the regular pattern and are able to work with success and confidence throughout the text.

Use in Small-Group or Class Situations

Although the books in the Adult Learner Series were designed primarily for use on an individual basis, they can be used successfully in small-group or class situations. The comprehension, language and life skills questions can be adapted to whole-class instruction; this may be especially useful for students of English as a Second Language. If several students have read the stories, a group discussion may prove rewarding as well as motivating.

Writing Assignments

The comprehension questions and answers may also serve as suggestions for writing assignments.

For many students at this level, a writing assignment must be introduced in a very structured manner; otherwise, some students may find themselves unable to get started. On a group basis, the writing assignment may grow naturally out of the class discussion. In this case, the discussion may be all the introduction necessary.

On an individual basis, however, and also often within a group situation, it will be necessary to provide the student with a more concrete starting point. The teacher may find it necessary to provide model sentences or paragraphs, or to supply sentence beginnings ("If I had been there, I would have . . .") for the student to complete. The students can use their copies of the stories to search for word spellings, or the teacher may wish to write suggested words on the blackboard or provide a prepared list.

The Word List

Every word used in the story is included in the Word List, given alphabetically under the chapter in which it is first introduced. New forms that are made by adding the suffixes *-s, -ed, -ing,* and *-ly* to words that have already been introduced are indented.

The instructor may wish to scan the Word List to choose preview words in addition to the twenty in the Preview Words section at the beginning of each chapter. Non-phonetic words, which may present some difficulties in decoding, are printed in italics for quick identification.

The Word List may also be used for the study of common sight words. Since an effort has been made to provide adequate repetition of each word, most of these words should be a solid part of the student's sight vocabulary by the time he or she has finished reading the story.

Summary of the Chapters in Peril on the Road

Chapter 1: On the Road (Level 3.5)

Rita and Jeff set out on their honeymoon, intending to ride cross-country from New York to San Francisco on Jeff's motorcycle, taking with them Rita's tiny dog, Mop. At their first campsite, they cross paths with two men in a van who evidently have something to hide.

Chapter 2: Get Out! (Level 3.2)

Jeff and Rita make a stop at the Chicago home of Rita's aunt and uncle. The men in the van spot them and begin to be afraid that the young couple are in fact police officers who are following them. They discuss a change of plans which would carry them farther north on their own trip to San Francisco. While at her aunt's house, Rita calls her mother and discovers that the museum where her mother works has been robbed of valuable paintings. Rita and Jeff discover that Mop makes them unwelcome guests, and leave earlier than they had planned, heading on the same northerly route as the van.

Chapter 3: The Badlands (Level 3.2)

Jeff and Rita make a stop in the South Dakota Badlands. They start out down a marked path, but Jeff chases Mop down a ravine and becomes lost. Rita locates him, and they push on to Mount Rushmore.

Chapter 4: Closing In (Level 3.0)

Rita and Jeff stop in Sheridan, Wyoming, to watch a rodeo, but Mop causes trouble in the ring, and they have to leave. The two robbers spot them and become even more sure that Jeff and Rita are following them. The men plot to kill them in their tent that night, but Mop frightens them off by barking.

Chapter 5: The Cobra Strikes (Level 3.0)

Rita and Jeff do some sight-seeing in Yellowstone Park. The robbers, Ken and Steve, steal a fast car and try to force the motorcycle over a cliff on the highway. Jeff manages to dodge them, and the car crashes. When Jeff and Rita return with help, there is no one in the car.

Chapter 6: The Last Move (Level 3.8)

Rita and Jeff push on into Oregon. Meanwhile, the two robbers retrieve their van and continue westward on the same road. When the motorcycle blows a tire, Jeff takes the wheel into town, leaving Rita alone by the side of a lonely road. Steve and Ken discover her there and try to force her into the van. Mop saves her by running out in front of a passing truck. Rita calls for the police on the truck's CB radio. Finally, in California, on the last evening of their journey, Jeff and Rita find a new puppy to take home with them in Mop's place.

Words Introduced in the Story

Non-phonetic words are in italics. New forms of words already introduced are indented.

Chapter 1: On the Road

a
about
across
added
after
afternoon
again
against
ago
ahead
all
almost
alone
along
already
always
and
another
any
anyone
anything
apartment
are
area
arm
  arms
around
as
asked
asleep
at
ate
aunt
away
back
bad
bags
bar
barked
  barking
be
been
before
behind
belong
bent
beside
best
better
between
big
  biggest
bike
  bikes
black
blowout
blue
boots
both
box
  boxes
breakfast
brown
bumper
but
buy
by
cake
California
called
  calling
came
camp
  camping
campfire
campground
campsite
can
can't
cared
carefully
changed
chapter
check
  checked
  checking
cheer
Chicago
chin
church
city
climbed
closed
  closely
  closing
clothes
coals
come
  comes
  coming
cooking

cops
corner
could
couldn't
count
country
course
crackling
crawled
crazy
cross
  crossed
cry
curled
cut
cute

dark
day
  days
did
didn't
do
  doing
does
doesn't
dog
  dogs
don't
done
door
  doors
down
dressed
drink
drive
  driver
drove
dust

each
ear
  ears
early
easy
eat
  eating
else
end
even
ever
every
everyone
everything
exit

faces
family
fast
  faster
feel
  feeling
  feels
feet
felt
few
find
fine
fire
first
flashed
flat
followed
food
footprints
for
forgot
found
friend
  friendly
  friends
from
front
funny
fur

gas
gave
gear
get
  getting
girl
give
  giving
glad
gleaming
glowed
go
  going
gone
good
got
grabbed
  grabbing
grass
great
grinning
ground
growled
guy

had
hadn't
hair
hand
  hands
happen
happy
has
have

he
head
  headed
  heads
hear
heard
heavy
held
hello
helmet
  helmets
her
here
hey
highway
hills
him
his
holding
home
honeymoon
hope
  hoped
hopped
how
hug
  hugged
hurry

I
  I'll
  I'm
  I've
if
in
idea
inside
into
Iowa
is
isn't

it
  it's
  its

jacket
  jackets
jeans
Jeff
  Jeff's
job
jumped
just

keep
Ken
kept
kicked
kickstand
kids
knew
  know

lap
last
later
laugh
  laughed
leaned
  leaning
leather
leave
  leaving
left
legs
let
  let's
life
light
like
  likes

line
  lines
little
lived
  lives
load
lock
long
look
  looked
  looking
lost
lot
  lots
loved
  loves

made
make
  making
man
many
married
match
matter
may
me
mean
meet
men
middle
miles
mind
mine
minute
Mom
moment
Monday
money
Mop/mop
  Mop's

more
morning
mother
motor
motorcycle
moving
much
must
mutt
my

name
near
Nebraska
Nevada
never
new
New Jersey
New York
next
nice
night
no
not
nothing
now

of
off
office
oh
OK
on
one
only
onto
open
  opened
  opens
other
our

out
over

packages
packed
  packing
paper
parked
  parking
part
passed
pat
  patting
peace
  peaceful
people
person
pick
  picked
pink
place
planned
  planning
  plans
plate
pockets
pointed
  pointing
poor
popped
postcard
power
presents
proudly
pull
  pulled
  pulling
put
  putting

quickly
quietly
quite

ran
reached
ready
really
relax
rest
ribbon
ride
  rides
right
Rita
  Rita's
river
road
roar
  roared
rode
rolled
rope
run
  running
rushing

sad
saddlebags
said
same
San Francisco
sat
Saturday
saw
say
  saying
seat
see
seemed
seen
send

set
setting
shaking
share
sharply
she
she's
short
should
shout
shouting
show
shut
side
sign
signs
signal
sissy
sitting
slammed
sleep
sleepily
sleeping
slowing
slowly
smells
sniffed
sniffing
so
some
someday
someone
something
sometimes
somewhere
soon
sorry
sound
sounds
speed
spent
stand
standing
start
started
state
states
stay
stayed
steal
Steve
stick
sticking
still
stood
stop
stopped
strange
streets
stretched
stretching
stuck
stuff
such
suddenly
supper
sure
swung

tail
take
taken
talk
talked
talking
tell
telling
tent
than
thanks
that
that's
the
their
them
then
there
there's
these
they
they're
they've
thing
things
think
thinking
this
those
thought
three
threw
through
tightly
time
tired
to
today
told
too
took
top
touring
toward
traffic
tried
trip
trips
try
trying

turn
turned
two

uncle
under
United States
unlocked
unzipped
us
Utah

van
very
voice

waist
wait
waiting
walk
walked
walking
want
wanted
was
wasn't
watch
watched
watching
waved
way
we
we'll
we're
we've
wedding
weeks
welcome
well
went
were
weren't
west
what
what's
when
where
which
while
who
why
wife
wife's
will
wind
window
winking
wished
with
without
woke
won't
wonder
wondered
wore
work
worry
would
wouldn't
Wyoming

Yamaha
years
yelled
yes
yet
you
you'll
you're
your

Chapter 2: Get Out!

able
allow
allowed
answering
asking
awful

baseball
basket
bathroom
bed
bedroom
began
bet
bought
broke
broken
broom
bums
burst

call
camped
car
catch
caught
chance

change
cheek
children
clean
clear
Cleveland
closet
closing
cloudy
coffee
colds
corn
counter
crash
cup
cups
cupboard

darling
dear
digging
dirt
dishes
doorbell
downstairs
dress
due

expect
extra

face
fall
far
fell
finished
fixed
floor
fly
flying

follow
following
fool
forward
four
fun
game
garage
grill

half
hall
hallway
hamburger
hamburgers
happened
happily
hard
harder
he'll
he's
help
helped
here's
highways
hood
hopefully
hours
house
housewife
hungry
hurried
hurt
hurting
husband

Idaho
Indiana

jumping

kid
kiss
kitchen

large
late
laughing
least
led
licked
licking
lie
lying
lifting
living
longer
lose
loud
loudly
love
lovely
lump
lunch

map
maybe
Meg
might
minutes
mouth
move
museum

nail
napkin
napkins
nasty
neat
neither
north

northern
not
nothing

Ohio
old
Oregon
outside

paintings
pale
past
  patted
peeked
Pennsylvania
phone
picnic
pictures
plane
plant
please
police
pot
proud
pour
pretty
pushed
  pushing

questions
  quick

rain
rang
  reaching
redwood
restaurant
rid
  riding
robbed
  robbers
room
route

sadly
safer
scare
scream
  screamed
sell
  shake
  she'll
shook
  shouted
sick
sisters
  sit
sky
smile
  smiled
  sniff
soft
  someone's
someplace
south
South Dakota
spilled
spoke
spotted
spread
stairs
station
  stays
stepped
stolen
stop
  stopped
straight
stupid
sun
Sunday

table
  taking
  they'll
thrown
thumbs
tickets
tie
tipped
tonight
trash
travel
trees
trucks
twenty

  uncle's
until
unzipping
upset
upstairs
use

waitress
wash
  washing
water
wear
  week
weekend
white
wig
  wishing
woman
wonderful
word
  worked
  working

works
worried
worth
wow
wrap
wrong
you'd
you've

Chapter 3: The Badlands

air
angrily
aren't
awhile

badlands
bark
beating
bench
bend
besides
bigger
bike's
blinked
bottom
boy
breath
bright
brightly
bumped

card
careful
cares
cars
carved
cliffs
climb
closer
colored
colors
cooler
covered

cream
crumbled

danger
deep
die
dizzy
dream
dropped
dry
dug

earth
easily
echo
echoed
edges
enough
everywhere
eyes

families
farther
fear
fishing
full

gasped
giant
grassland
grasslands
grow
guys

herself
hide
higher
hill
himself
hot
hugging
humming
hundred

ice
Illinois

jug

kept
kind

lakes
land
listened

mad
mailbox
main
mile
millions
monument
mostly
Mount Rushmore
mountain
myself

need
needed
noise
note

once
openings
others

path
pine
play
point
poured

rags
ravine
ravines
read
remember
rising
roaring
rock
rocks
roll
rolling
rushed

sang
seek
seems
shade
shadow
shining
shoulders
showed
showing
shrugged
sides
sight
sip
smaller
smart
snapped
sometime
song
stamp
steep
stirring
striped
stripes
strong
stuffed
sun
sunlight

tall
tasted
thirsty
tied
together
ton
tons
tools
trailers
turning
twisted
twisting

unrolling
used

vans

waited
wall
warm
western
whole
wide
wing
wish
woods
works
world
worn
wrote

zipped

Chapter 4: Closing In

alongside
American
anger
angry
anywhere
ask
awfully
backed
bang
barks
because
beginning
being
believe
bird
body
breathing
bringing
bull
bull's
bulls

campfires
campsites
cards
carry
carried
carving
chase
cheered
cheering
circle
close
cloud
clown
clowns
clutching
collar
cow
cows
cowboys
crowd
crowds
cruised
cruising
cuts

danced
dancing
dangerous
darned
driver's
dying

edge

fat
fighting
finally
finger
flash
flashlight
flew
free

gets
grandstand

hat
hats
having
heading
herds
hid
hiding
high
hit
holed
hooves
huge
hung
hurrying

Indian
it'll

jump

kicking
knife
knows

landed
lay
lifted
liked
loaded
looks
losing
lucky

makes
matter
met
miss
missed
most
mountains
moved

nearby
neck
necklace
necklaces
nodded

overheat
own

painted
painting
park
party
passing
picking
pounded
pounding

quiet

race
railing
raised
reading
remembering
ring
robbery
rodeo
rodeos
rubbed

saving
scrambling
seats
sheep
Sheridan
shined
shirt
sidewalk
silver
since
sir
slid
slip
sold
sounded
space
spot
stab
Steve's
stopping
store
stores
straining

street
string
sudden

thank
throttle
tight
times
tiny
tomorrow
touched
trouble
twist

unzip
upset

wake
wakes
waving
wild
windows
wings
woof

yawning
Yellowstone

Chapter 5: The Cobra Strikes

alive
anyway
aunt's

baby
barn
bit
blast
blows
brand
break
bubble
bubbles
builds
bushes

camera
cameras
care
cliff
climbing
clutch
Cobra
couple
crashed
crossing
crowded
cutting

dare
deeper

eggs
empty

famous
fight
five
foot
forcing

goes
guard

hang
hate
hidden
hold
hole
hour

I'd

Ken's
kill
knees
known

lean
less
lights
longer
lower

mask
mirror
mud

nose
now's
nowhere

package
pass
pavement
picture
plan
policeman
policemen
pow
push

rails
ranch
ranger
ranger's
rangers
reach
rear
report
rescue
rotten
rumble

scared
screeching
seem
sent
shaky
shifter
shot
shouldn't
sights
skid
skidded
slowed
smell
smelled
smiling
springs
squeezed
staring
steam
straw
strikes
sweat

tall
tap
thinks
third
tires
tow
train
trees
truck

we'd
wheel
wildly
wrecked

Chapter 6: The Last Move

acting
Atlantic

badly
ball
banged
bat
beach
beaches
bite
blew
blow
bones
brakes
bridge
buttons

case
clinging
coast
cold
cooked
cool

dead
dragged
dragging
driving

east
eye

fault
fix
fixing

floppy
fog
footsteps
forget

gang
gasping
growl
growling
gulp
gun

hangs
hardly
hears
hop
hope
hopped

instead

lady
laid
leg
lit

man's
mike
mops
motel

nearest
newspapers

ocean
often
ones
outdoors

Pacific
pack
pain
pancakes
pants
playing
poking
pool
puppy
puppies

radio
real
rubbing

saddlebag
safe
saved
shorter
six
sleeping
smoothly
softly
spare
spinning
spot
step
stole
stops
story

tears
themselves
throw
tire
town
trailer
trained
trunk
tucked
turns

unless

waded
wave
wreck

Answer Key

Comprehension Questions

Chapter 1

1. b	2. b	3. d	4. a	5. b
6. d	7. d	8. c	9. a	10. c

Chapter 2

1. c	2. c	3. b	4. d	5. c
6. c	7. b	8. d	9. a	10. a

Chapter 3

1. b	2. c	3. d	4. b	5. a
6. a	7. d	8. b	9. d	10. a

Chapter 4

1. d	2. b	3. c	4. c	5. d
6. a	7. c	8. b	9. b	10. a

Chapter 5

1. a	2. b	3. c	4. a	5. c
6. d	7. d	8. b	9. c	10. d

Chapter 6

1. b	2. b	3. d	4. d	5. c
6. a	7. c	8. b	9. a	10. b

Language Skills

Chapter 1: Exercise 1

1. The Smiths have a new baby girl, and the Greenbergs have a baby boy.
2. We are eating chicken at the picnic, and they are eating hamburgers.
3. Are you moving into your new house on Saturday, or will you wait until Monday?
4. Cara wanted to take a trip to Florida, but she did not have enough money.
5. I will get the tools, and Janice will change the oil in my car.
6. Beverly waited a few more minutes, and then she decided to go on by herself.
7. I would like to take the children to the zoo, but I have to work this weekend.
8. Andy will visit you on Sunday, and Sam will drop by on Monday.

Exercise 2

1. Do you want to wash the dishes, or do you want to dry them?
2. Ann is a carpenter, and Shelly is a banker.
3. We take our baby to Dr. Mendez, but they take their baby to Dr. Jackson.
4. I like to go sailing, but I often get seasick.
5. Where will you go on vacation, and what will you do there?
6. Donnie can play the piano, but he can't read music.
7. We can eat ice cream at home, or we can go out for banana splits.
8. Linda said she would come with us, but I do not see her anywhere.
9. Keep the pot covered, and bring the water to a boil.

Chapter 2: Exercise 1

1. Our family has one dog, two cats, three birds, and two turtles.
2. Kate gave me a rake, a spade, and a hoe.
3. Pick up eggs, oranges, bread, and milk at the supermarket.
4. You can get books, records, and tapes at our library.
5. Tom was wearing a gray suit, a light blue shirt, and a blue-striped tie.
6. We packed toothbrushes, toothpaste, soap, shampoo, and razors in our suitcases.

Exercise 2

1. Today I must buy food, bake a cake, and cook dinner.
2. Carmen got in the car, put on her seatbelt, started the engine, and drove down the street.
3. I need an oil pan, a wrench, an oil filter, and three cans of oil to change the oil in my car.
4. Please wash the dishes, wipe off the table, and sweep the floor.
5. Tomorrow I am leaving work early, catching the 3:00 train, and going to Dallas.
6. Mary Lou put stars, angels, and colored lights on her Christmas tree.
7. A waitress must take the order, serve the food, remove the dishes, and give the bill to the customer.

Chapter 3: Exercise 1

1. "I already put gas in the car," said Roberta.
2. Steve said, "You can stay at our house."
3. "My son is getting a dog for his birthday," said Danny.
4. "I made these curtains myself," said Mike.

5. Jesse said, "We will pick you up at 8:30 in the morning."
6. "I will check the football standings in the paper," said Anita.
7. Ralph asked, "Is the mall open on Sundays?"
8. Paul said, "I never learned to swim."
9. "Be careful crossing the street," Lucia said.

Exercise 2

1. "I want some ice cream," said Brenda.
   Brenda said, "I want some ice cream."
2. "Turn off the TV," said Bill.
   Bill said, "Turn off the TV."
3. "Our house was just painted," said Deanna.
   Deanna said, "Our house was just painted."
4. "You can take the eight o'clock bus," said Lisa.
   Lisa said, "You can take the eight o'clock bus."
5. "Have some more salad," David said.
   David said, "Have some more salad."
6. "I earned a lot of money last year," said Christina.
   Christina said, "I earned a lot of money last year."

Chapter 4: Exercise 1

1. It is time for bed, Jackie.
2. Kathy, turn off the stove.
3. Where is your purse, Jean?
4. Dad, can I go to the party?
5. Watch your step, Kevin.
6. Did you make the cake, Suzanne?
7. Rick, wait for me!

Exercise 2

1. Matt, eat your pie.
   Eat your pie, Matt.

2. David, it's your turn now.
   It's your turn now, David.
3. Katie, have you met Susan?
   Have you met Susan, Katie?
4. Mona, stay in the house.
   Stay in the house, Mona.
5. Son, make your bed.
   Make your bed, son.
6. Ron, did you feed the baby?
   Did you fed the baby, Ron?
7. Will, it is time to go.
   It is time to go, Will.

Chapter 5: Exercise 1

1. April 12, 1963
2. Sunday, April 12, 1963
3. Friday, December 6
4. June 6, 1978
5. Thursday, May 30, 1966
6. November 14, 1938

Exercise 2:

1. My sister was born on Thursday, July 1, 1958.
2. Monday, June 13 is Janet's graduation day.
3. This year we will celebrate Martin Luther King's birthday on Monday, January 15.
4. We moved to Texas on Friday, May 22, 1955.
5. Can you finish the job by Saturday, April 11?
6. Wednesday, July 4 is a holiday for the whole family.

Exercise 3

1. Trafalgar Square, London, England
2. 14 Locust Street, Burlington, Vermont
3. Toronto, Ontario

4. Grant Avenue, San Francisco, California, United States of America

Exercise 4

1. André lives in Paris, France.
2. Sally drove to Santa Fe, New Mexico.
3. Have you ever been to London, England?
4. Bogotá, Colombia is a large city.
5. My address is 55 Blake Street, Fort Wayne, Indiana.

Chapter 6: Exercise 1

1. Place Name
2. Date
3. List of Items
4. Direct Address
5. Place Name
6. Compound Sentence
7. Quotation
8. Compound Sentence

Exercise 2

1.	We bring pencils, paper, and books to class.	List of Items
2.	When will you come, Wendy?	Direct Address
3.	Marcia said, "I like pizza."	Quotation
4.	I leave for Africa on Thursday, July 2.	Date
5.	We need candy, soda, ice cream, and cake for the party.	List of Items
6.	My son is six years old, and my daughter is five.	Compound Sentence
7.	Cindy comes from Boise, Idaho.	Place Name
8.	Help me pack, Fred.	Direct Address

Understanding Life Skills

Chapter 1

1. benches, chairs, sofas, tables
2. Bedding
3. Raincoats
4. Pillows

Chapter 2

No questions included

Chapter 3

No questions included

Chapter 4

Alabama
4¢ on every dollar
110.00
No

Chapter 5

113.1-14 lbs.
2.14
$30.01-50.00
$4.25

Chapter 6

J.C. Penney Catalog Division
P.O. Box 6231
Reno, Nevada 89599

Applying Life Skills

Chapter 1: Exercise 1

1. Men's Wear
2. Jewelry
3. Sporting Goods
4. Luggage
5. Men's Wear
6. Sporting Goods
7. Sporting Goods
8. Jewelry

Exercise 2

1. Rings
2. Shoes
3. Ski Clothing
4. Sweaters
5. Tools

Exercise 3

1. 496
2. 460
3. 36
4. 241
5. 639
6. 655
7. 53
8. 416

Chapter 2

1. a. E
   b. rayon canvas with vinyl trim
   c. brown and black
   d. 82
   e. Z-649
   f. 7.7 lbs.
   g. 49.75

2. a. G
   b. rayon-cotton blend
   c. by machine in warm water
   d. small, medium, large
   e. 6930
   f. 1 lb.
   g. 9.00

3. a. A
   b. 180 watts
   c. R-785
   d. 16.5 lbs.
   e. 29.99

4. a. C
   b. steel
   c. friction brake
   d. 343
   e. 5 lbs.
   f. 35.00

Chapter 3: Exercise 1

PAGE NUMBER	NAME OF ITEM	CATALOG NUMBER letter	CATALOG NUMBER number	SIZE	COLOR (name & number)	HOW MANY	PRICE dollars	PRICE cents	WEIGHT
67	Wingback armchair	R	792	—	sea green 82	1	260	00	50 lbs.

Exercise 2

1. 28.99 2.2
2. 183.00 6.9
3. 72.75 18.6
4. 201.00 30.1

Chapter 4: Exercise 1

1. a. 4¢ on every dollar
   b. No Tax
2. a. No Tax
   b. 5¢ on every dollar
3. a. 5¢ on every dollar
   b. 5¢ on every dollar
   c. No Tax
   d. 4¢ on every dollar

Exercise 2

1. 3½¢ on every dollar
2. 5¢ on every dollar
3. 5¢ on every dollar
4. No Tax
5. 5½¢ on every dollar

Chapter 5: Exercise 1

1. 26.1-27 lbs. 2.89
2. 37.1-38 lbs. 3.54
3. 14.1-15 lbs. 2.19
4. 11.1-12 lbs. 2.05

Exercise 2

1. over $100.00 $6.00
2. over $100.00 $6.00
3. $30.01-$50.00 $4.25
4. $15.01-$30.00 $3.00

Chapter 6: Exercise 1

☑ **Check Method of Payment**

☐ **I have enclosed a check or money order.**

☑ **Charge to my:** master charge (THE INTERBANK CARD) / VISA (circled)
(Circle one)

Card #: 5141 102 881 375

Expiration date: 08 92

Student's signature
Signature (as shown on credit card)

Exercise 2

1. Sears Catalog Center
   Boston, MA 02215
2. Sears Catalog Center
   Seattle, WA 98184
3. Sears Catalog Center
   Los Angeles, CA 90051
4. Sears Catalog Center
   Memphis, TN 38140
5. Sears Catalog Center
   Chicago, IL 60607

Exercise 3

1. 130
2. striped sweater
3. large
4. 80 gray/pink
5. Z 271-31
6. $27.00
7. $29.58
8. 61852034651

Comprehension Progress Graph

How to Use the Comprehension Progress Graph

1. At the top of the graph, find the number of the chapter you have just read.
2. Follow the line down until it crosses the line for the number of questions you got right.
3. Put a dot • where the lines cross.
4. The numbers on the other side of the graph show your comprehension score.

For example, this graph shows the score of a student who answered 7 questions right for Chapter 1. The score is 70%.

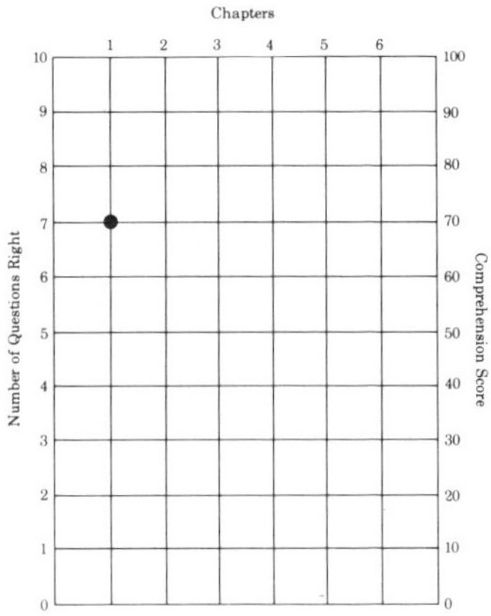

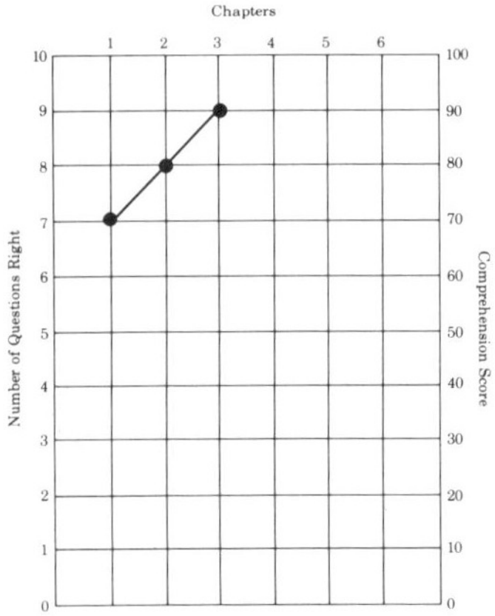

This same student got scores of 80% and 90% on Chapters 2 and 3. The line connecting the dots keeps going up. This shows that the student is doing well.

If the line between the dots on your graph does not go up, or if it goes down, see your instructor for help.

Comprehension Progress

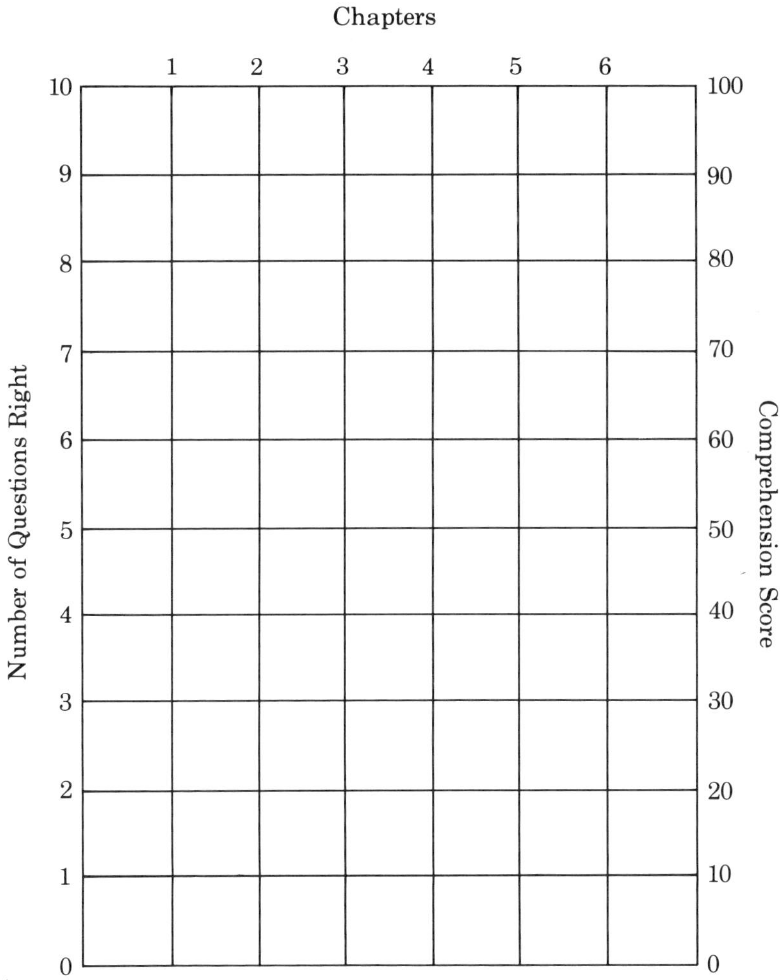

Skills Profile Graph

How to Use the Skills Profile Graph

1. There is a block on this graph for every comprehension question in the book.
2. Every time you get a question wrong, fill in a block which has the same letter as the question you got wrong. For example, if you get an A question wrong, fill in a block in the A row. Use the right row for each letter.

Look at the graph. It shows the profile of a student who got 3 questions wrong. This student got an A question wrong, a C question wrong, and a D question wrong.

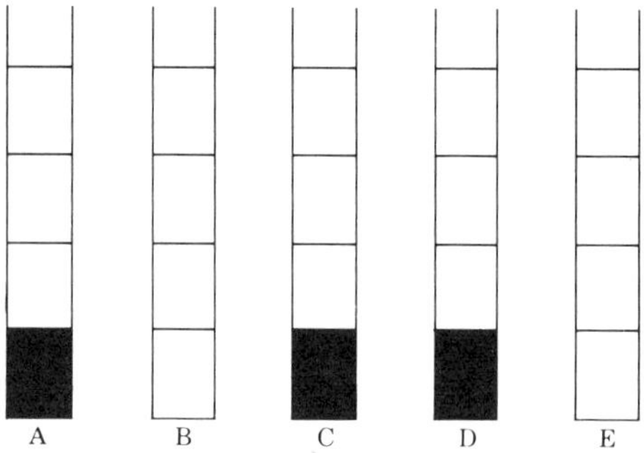

In the next chapter, this same student got 4 questions wrong and has filled in 4 more blocks.

The graph now looks like this. This student seems to be having trouble on question C. This shows a reading skill that needs to be worked on.

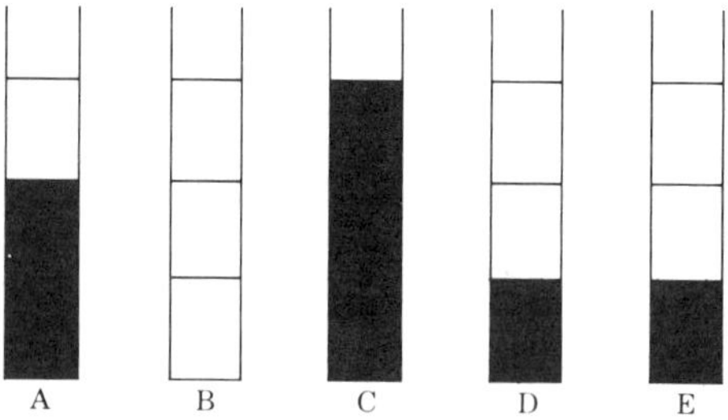

The blocks that are filled in on your graph tell you and your instructor the kinds of questions that give you trouble.

Look for the rows that have the most blocks filled in.

These rows will be higher than the others. Talk to your instructor about them. Your instructor may want to give you extra help on these skills.

Skills Profile

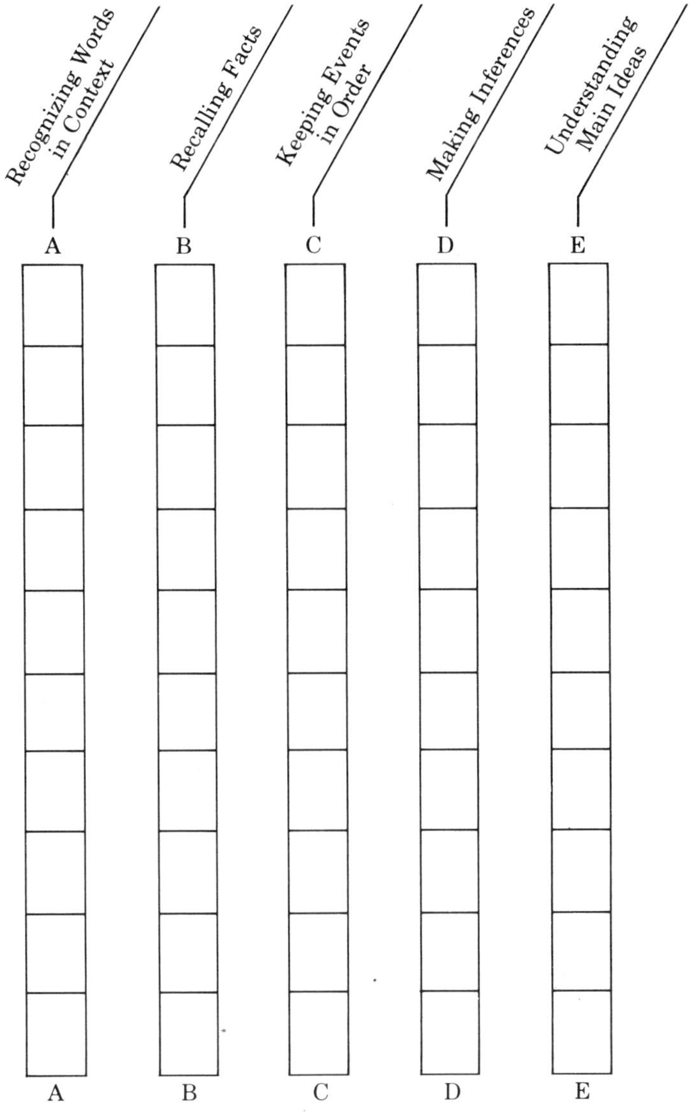